What the critics are saying…

5 flames "This story was action-packed and steamy hot from page one. It was like a movie, but instead I was reading it. EXCELLENT READ! GO OUT AND GET IT ASAP!" ~ *Kelly Sizzling Romances*

WOW! "I don't have any words to describe Lord Of The Deep. It's by far the best book in The Horde Wars series so far…this book has made me speechless—so just get this book!" ~ *Raven, Mon-Boudoir reviews*

"Sherri L. King's books just keep getting better and better. I am in awe of her incredible talent. She has created an impressive world … that will awe any fan of paranormal novels. LORD OF THE DEEP has been much anticipated and it does not disappoint! If you haven't yet read these, run and buy them all. You will not regret becoming immersed in this amazing world." ~ *Nicole Hulst, eCataRomance Reviews*

SHERRI L. KING

LORD OF THE DEEP

ELLORA'S CAVE
ROMANTICA PUBLISHING

An Ellora's Cave Romantica Publication

www.ellorascave.com

Lord of the Deep

ISBN #1419951645
ALL RIGHTS RESERVED.
Lord of the Deep Copyright© 2004 Sherri L. King
Edited by: Heather Osborn
Cover art by: Darrell King

Electronic book Publication: July, 2004
Trade paperback Publication: April, 2005

Excerpt from *Fetish* Copyright © Sherri L. King, 2004
Excerpt from *Beyond Illusion* Copyright © Sherri L. King, 2005

Warning:

The following material contains graphic sexual content meant for mature readers. *Lord of the Deep* has been rated *E-rotic* by a minimum of three independent reviewers.

Ellora's Cave Publishing offers three levels of Romantica™ reading entertainment: S (S-ensuous), E (E-rotic), and X (X-treme).

S-*ensuous* love scenes are explicit and leave nothing to the imagination.

E-*rotic* love scenes are explicit, leave nothing to the imagination, and are high in volume per the overall word count. In addition, some E-rated titles might contain fantasy material that some readers find objectionable, such as bondage, submission, same sex encounters, forced seductions, etc. E-rated titles are the most graphic titles we carry; it is common, for instance, for an author to use words such as "fucking", "cock", "pussy", etc., within their work of literature.

X-*treme* titles differ from E-rated titles only in plot premise and storyline execution. Unlike E-rated titles, stories designated with the letter X tend to contain controversial subject matter not for the faint of heart.

Also by Sherri L. King:

Lord of the Deep

The Horde Wars

For Darrell, my one.

Thanks to Crissy and to Mark, who saved me from the depths of those dark waters with a life jacket and a turkey sandwich.

"And of Amphitrite and the loud-roaring Earth-Shaker Poseidon was born great, wide-ruling Triton, and he owns the depths of the sea...an awful god." ~ *Theogony 930*

"Every time we walk along a beach some ancient urge disturbs us so that we find ourselves shedding shoes and garments or scavenging among seaweed and whitened timbers like the homesick refugees of a long war." ~ *Loren Eiseley*

For whatever we lose (like a your or a me),

"It's always our self we find in the sea." ~ *E.E. Cummings*

"You are a child of the universe no less than the trees and the stars; you have a right to be here. And whether or not it is clear to you, no doubt the universe is unfolding as it should. Therefore be at peace with God, whatever you conceive him to be. And whatever your labors and aspirations, in the noisy confusion of life, keep peace in your soul. With all its sham, drudgery and broken dreams, it is still a beautiful world." ~ *Desiderata*

Prologue

Her name is Niki Akitoye. No matter what happens, you can't let her be taken. She's far too powerful, far too dangerous to let slip into enemy hands. It's my fault I didn't tell you sooner but…it's so hard to think clearly here…

Grimm looked around, puzzled. Those words…they'd been spoken in Raine's voice. But where was she? And where was *he*? He couldn't see anything through the blasted fog that surrounded him and flooded his vision.

Reaper, are you listening to me? Raine sounded impatient now.

"I can't see you," he murmured softly, almost afraid that if he dared to speak any louder, the dream might end and Raine's ghost would be lost to him again.

You don't need to see me to hear me, stupid. Besides, I don't have the energy to spare you a vision just now, but what I have to say is very important so listen, really listen to what I'm saying. You have to reach Niki before the Daemons do. If you fail, the Shikars are very likely fucked.

Grimm's heart lurched and he squared his shoulders against the weakness, straightening to his full height, an imposing six feet ten inches. If Raine wanted this woman Niki Akitoye found, he would find her. If Raine warned that the Shikars' safety was at stake should the woman not be found…he would turn the world upside down to save his people, reach into the very heart of Hell to find Niki before the Daemon Horde could.

Don't get your back up just yet. You've still got time to get to her before the Daemons do. But first—this is very important—you must find Tryton. I don't know why, but he really needs to be there with you when you find her, and you need every advantage you can get, whatever that may be. If you hurry, you can just catch him—he's on a commercial fishing boat in Alaska. Find him and save the girl. Do it as fast as you can, everything depends on this.

Grimm caught a faint whiff of her light floral scent in the damp, stagnant air of the psychic-world that surrounded him. He tried to track it, track her, but no matter how he concentrated, how much of his considerable power he used, she remained elusive. Either she didn't want him to find her, or she simply wasn't there to be found.

Quit wasting time, Grimm! I'm not the one you should be concerned about just now. She is. Her name is Niki Akitoye. She'll be on an airplane crossing the Mississippi in less than twenty-four hours. After that, it'll probably be too late. Go. Find her and save her. Please.

So many times this woman had helped the Shikars in their fight against the Daemons. For whatever purpose, her heart was with the Shikar Alliance now, and she protected them whenever she could. Who was he to refuse such an ardent request from one such as she? There was nothing Raine could ask for that he would not move heaven and hell to give.

"I'll find Tryton and I *will* save Niki," he vowed solemnly. "But how will I find you again?" He had to know.

She laughed abruptly, but the sound was lacking all warmth and amusement. Instead it was dull and lifeless. Bereft of all hope. It chilled him to hear so desolate a sound from her. Made him shudder down to his very bones.

Her laughter ceased as quickly as it had begun. *I'll find you, Reaper. Never fear about that. I'll find you when I need you.*

The fog began to dissipate, and blackness took its place in his vision and his heart. The presence that was Raine was leaving, and with it went all the light and warmth in his world.

"Damn you, woman. What if I need you?" he roared, all the pain and rage he felt echoing in his cry.

You don't need anyone, Grimm. You never have. You never will...

But he did. Desperately, tragically, he did need someone.

He needed *her*. He needed Raine. More and more, with each passing night.

But Raine was dead. And nothing, not even his own considerable power, could ever change that horrible, tragic fact.

Chapter One

"Keep your eyes closed, Miranda. It won't be much longer."

"I feel so warm," the ailing woman sighed, and at last the suffering eased from her strained face.

"But do you still feel the pain?"

"No," her voice was full of wonder. "No, I don't."

Niki grinned, but it was more a baring of teeth than a real smile. She focused all her energies on Miranda's stomach. It was being eaten away by cancer, just as her doctors had diagnosed. But soon...soon, it might not be anymore. If she could just focus a little while longer.

Miranda jerked on the daybed where she was reclined, and Niki moved in to make the last strike that she hoped would end her patient's suffering. This final, great push should decimate the invading cells that ate at Miranda's body like a hungry monster. A monster that never slept, never rested, and always fed its endless appetite.

Niki pushed that last thought aside, shuddering at the lapse, losing a tiny bit of her control.

"*Ooooh*," Miranda moaned. "That hurts."

"Not much longer now." Niki refocused and pushed her healing magic into the woman's frail body once again.

How she had this power was a mystery to her. But she had ideas, ideas that terrified and shamed her and made her wake up in a cold sweat each night. Niki would probably never know the real answers, and that was fine enough by her, they were no doubt just as terrifying as her nightmares. This power was both a gift and a curse, one that had nearly ruined her life and the lives of those around her.

But now she believed that she had some sort of handle on the situation that had once been so desperate and dangerous. In the beginning, when she'd first discovered her empathic talents, she'd been unable to control them. Years had passed since then, painful, desperate times, but she'd developed some small measure of self-possession that now enabled her to keep the power in check. So long as she didn't encounter situations that evoked any great passion or anger, she was fine.

And everyone around her stayed alive and well.

"So warm," the woman sighed again, easier this time.

Niki felt the heat herself. Felt and saw the soft, golden light that flowed in a thrumming current from her to her patient. "Keep your eyes tightly closed, Miranda," she warned. It wouldn't do to have Miranda see this strange phenomenon. It wouldn't do at all.

Niki had learned early on that her patients tended to freak out completely when they saw this golden glow infusing them. They could accept her miraculous healing powers—but only in a very limited capacity. They could somewhat accept the unexplainable success rate she had with numerous other clients—despite the laws of science and medicine. They could even, to some degree, overlook how impossible such a thing should be, her ability to heal even the most hopeless cases with but a few visits like this one. But none of them could ever accept that what she did was, undeniably, magical.

Miracles were common enough to be believed apparently, especially medical miracles. It was almost a triumph, for most patients, to be able to tell their overpriced doctors that their death march was finally over and it had nothing to do with their medicines or their outlandish treatments.

But one whiff of anything supernatural, genuinely supernatural that is, and everyone panicked. Seeing was believing, it seemed, and the sight of such things like the healing light in Niki's hands terrified everyone—even Niki herself in the beginning. Better no one saw the proof of the magic. Better they keep their eyes closed tight against the light. It had taken Niki several abrupt relocations, fleeing from one incredulous town to another, to figure that one out.

The majority of her clients held on to the desperate belief that, though Niki claimed to be a psychic healer, it was mostly luck that she ever succeeded in what she did. When asked, most of them would say she was an eccentric quack—no matter how horrible a disease they had survived with Niki's help. Deep down, no one really wanted to believe the truth. In fact, they were afraid to.

Niki knew this was merely human nature, to discard any proof of the supernatural so that they didn't have to face the reality of—and therefore the problem of dealing with—its existence. Niki accepted this. Hell, she wanted to deny her own powers most of the time...oh, if only she could.

Miranda, the woman she tended to now, would be no different from all the rest. She would be so grateful at first, once she knew for certain that the cancer was gone. But soon after would come the doubts. And after she'd spoken to friends and family, she would firmly believe that it was either God or fate or simply chance that had enabled her to beat the odds allowed by her awful illness. She would try her best to forget the strange warmth of Niki's touch. She would look away whenever she passed this house in her car. And if ever Miranda should see Niki in public, she would pointedly ignore her and walk away from any chance of meeting or confrontation.

Such things used to make Niki sad, or even angry. But now she just accepted them and moved on to the next patient, the next miracle, the next alienation.

Miranda sighed again, her breathing slowing even more as she easing fully into a trancelike state that Niki had come to expect. This odd trance, this restful hypnosis, meant that the healing session should end very soon. If Niki were to feed too much more of her power into the ailing woman, it might very well reverse any progress she had made. The human body could only withstand so much of this kind of healing before it rebelled.

Sometimes Niki saw this as an affirmation that her powers were not necessarily a good thing, no matter how hard she tried to use them in positive ways. If the human body rebelled against it — did her powers not then stand outside the very laws of nature? But at other times, Niki almost believed that this meant nothing. Nothing, perhaps, but that the human body was somewhat frail, and that maybe her power was just too strong for such delicate creatures to withstand.

It would explain the deaths.

No.

She refused to think about those just now. She spent far too much time dwelling on them as it was.

With a few final waves of heat that washed from her hands and straight into Miranda's distended stomach, Niki eased her patient from her trance with gentle words. Miranda blinked rapidly, her breathing still deep, but no longer slow, no longer halting. She awoke with a soft, vacant smile on her lips.

"Did I sleep?" the woman asked, still dazed.

"Yeah," Niki lied easily, "I think you did."

* * * * *

Niki sat on her front porch long after her patient had driven away. Miranda had been in a euphoric haze of wonder and relief that the horrible pains she'd endured for so many months now had abated. Niki knew that soon, eventually, the wonder would change to skepticism or even a mild sort of horror.

Oh well.

Niki hugged her bent legs tight, resting her chin on her knees, a grim tight line about her mouth. Her body hurt a little bit. It sometimes did after a healing session. But the aches weren't bad enough to inspire any effort on her part to get up and go take a couple of aspirin for it. The sultry heat and perfume of the swamp that flanked her property lulled and relaxed her in a way that no medicine ever could as she sat and brooded upon her porch deck.

The house was small and a rental, but it felt like home. More than any house, apartment, or trailer ever had in the past few years. This was where she'd been born and raised after all, here in the lush overgrowth of Savannah, Georgia. She felt an affinity for this place, for the land and for the climate, and she felt welcome, as if the very earth called out a soothing melody to her aching soul, asking her to stay for a while.

This land could keep its secrets. This seemingly stagnant stretch of swamp and weeping willows and Spanish moss had no memory of a time without ghosts and regrets. It was ripe with decay...but each rotting bough, each algae-eaten pond, each heavy secret kept for a hundred years or more was a symphony of new creation and life and fertility. Even the ghosts sought rebirth, in some form or fashion, through contact with the living. Niki often felt exactly the same way.

She loved it here. Always had. Always would — and she knew it. No matter how many times she moved away, no matter how far she strayed, she would always come back here, sooner or later. To recharge her spirit. To reinvigorate her soul. Savannah was her haven, when all other harbors of safety were spent.

But she'd eventually have to move again, and soon. Niki was almost certain that the year she'd spent here healing the sick and mending the injured was far too long a time to stay in one place. People talked. Rumors flew, as well as the truth — which was almost as damning as any fictitious story. It wouldn't be long now before the modern day witch-hunt began.

Fucking media. Inevitably it seemed they always caught wind of her and her accomplishments. Then one thing would lead to another and all her past encounters with reporters would surface and all her patients' lives would be interrupted by interview after interview and then the circus would be back in town. Niki wasn't naïve enough to believe that she could escape it this time if she stayed, any better than she had all the previous times she'd spent too long in one place.

Savannah was a bigger city now than it had been when she'd been a little girl. But it still possessed a small-town mentality, enough for talk of Niki Akitoye and her healing hands to spread far and wide amongst the people who lived here.

It was time to think about where she should go next.

Niki hugged her legs tighter, eyes painfully dry and wide. She'd spent all her tears by now. She was so tired of the race. So tired of the running. She felt like crying, felt like sobbing her problems into the deep, dark earth of the swamp's muddy banks. But the tears could not come. Her secrets were hers to keep still. The land here had enough of its own to sustain it until she returned. Again. And again. Until she was an old woman, too frail to run anymore. She'd always come back here.

Unless she got lucky and died along the way…*bah*. She was immediately ashamed of that thought and shook it from the cobwebs in her mind.

The phone rang shrilly, the call of it piercing through the screen door of her kitchen. With a slow, heavy sigh, she unfolded her body and went to see what bill collector was calling this time.

Chapter Two

The waves that lapped against the bow of the boat fascinated Tryton. Hypnotic and endless, they danced in countless different patterns, each a work of art and magic that rippled on into infinity. He wanted nothing more than to step off the ship and sink down, down, down, into the blue-black depths of the sea. To let the waves and the water envelop him like a warm, wet lover that would never stray, never die, never let him go. Let him sleep in peace beneath the sun and the moon and the wide expanse of sky.

The sun was sinking low upon the horizon, casting a blanket of molten gold and crimson across the water. Oh how he had missed the sun. It had been far too many years since he'd basked in the warmth and the light, and he'd forgotten how incredible, how magical the day could be. He'd dwelled in darkness for so long…but now, for a short while, he was free to join the day once again.

The sweet salt of the air tickled his senses. He breathed deep the crisp perfume and held it in his lungs for as long as he could stand it before exhaling once again. How he loved it here. How he wished he could stay exactly like this forever.

But he of all beings knew that nothing, absolutely nothing, could last forever.

Tryton leaned out farther over the deck railing, looking hard into the depths of the blue ocean water. Slowly, he reached forth with his hand, extended his index finger, and traced lazy whorls into the air. The water reflected the motion, then mimicked it exactly. It began to spin and twirl, gently arching up in long slender tendrils of liquid that tangled and spun into elaborate designs — like knots or lacework made of fine glass, longingly reaching for his fingers as they danced.

If anyone else on the mammoth Alaskan fishing boat had seen such a thing they would have been frightened or doubtful of their own sanity. There would be an outcry. No one would believe the ravings of the witness, the shrieks about magic and dancing water. But Tryton would have had to make his stay very short indeed, for he was already regarded as a strange and mysterious man among the other crew members.

With a last smooth wave of his hand, Tryton released his control of the dancing water, watched it fall with a splash back into the ocean, and sighed wearily. He knew it was almost time to go back home. He could feel it, like a tic beneath his eye. He'd spent far too much time away already. There were so many loose ends that needed tying up before he could disappear again. Truly disappear. He needed to get back and see that everything was prepared for his "death".

And how long would he stay dead this time? How long would it take his people to forget about him, so that when he reappeared again it would be as if he were a stranger — a lost warrior that had been separated from his people by some chance or mistake? How many times had he done this already? He could no longer remember.

Far too many times to count, that was how many times.

Perhaps this time his people wouldn't need him to come back. Maybe this time he could stay dead for good.

The Daemon Horde had been dealt a very serious blow, their ranks greatly diminished, their leader missing for many long centuries, maybe even dead. Without Lord Daemon to raise their ranks, the monsters had no source of power, no spark of life. Perhaps now, with victory inevitable, Tryton could truly rest. His people no longer needed him in this fight. He was ready to let them go.

And he was so tired. So very tired of this endless struggle.

The world of humans was so large, so vast, that he could simply disappear into it forever with none the wiser if he wished to. What a dream. What a life he could lead, in secret and in peace. But always there was this feeling of responsibility and debt to his people. He was largely the cause of the many long centuries of chaos and unrest after all. If not for him, the Shikars might still be part of the surface world, part of the land of sunlight.

No, he could not abandon them. He would not. He owed them so much. This life of war and struggle that the Shikars led was his fault. He would always be there to help them.

Unfortunately for him, always was a long, long time. He supposed he could take his own life…but that would be dishonorable and he was nothing if not a slave to his own honor. He should have died eons ago. But he hadn't. Now he feared that he was a true immortal. Whatever he'd done in that past, he'd paid in full and then some…and yet still he lived. He might very well live until the end of the world.

This was his greatest fear. And his fondest wish. He loved life after all, truly he did. He just hated the war and the strife that came with it. For no matter how old he was, no matter how wise he should have become over the years, he still made mistakes. And he dearly felt the cost of each and every one of them.

The cool spray of the water splashed against the warmth of his sun-darkened face, carried to him on a sudden, strong gust of wind. Damn it all, he wanted the embrace of that water. He wanted the long, healing sleep. It had been so long since the last time. The water called to him, like all the sweet, delicious lovers he'd been unable to resist over the years. The water promised him peace, for however long he should need it. He could not resist.

He climbed up onto the railing, closed his eyes and held his face high into the last fading rays of the sun, and calmly stepped off.

A strong hand clamped down upon his shoulder.

Tryton's eyes flew open and stung, but the stinging had nothing to do with the wind or the sea spray. He felt such overwhelming emotions that he almost struggled against the delaying hand.

But he didn't.

Tryton knew he was well and truly caught. Damn it. There would be no quiet solace in the water. No lazy walk upon the ocean floor as he'd enjoyed so many times in the past, looking over the ruins of ancient cities he'd helped to build. No gentle embrace of liquid. No sleep.

No rest.

The Shikars needed him, called to him. And there was nothing he could do but go to them.

The scent of the salt spray and the warmth of the sun disappeared entirely, replaced with the cold, endless burden of his duty. Of his destiny.

"Hello Grimm," Tryton sighed, the soft sound taken on a breeze and carried off to somewhere far away.

"Hello my friend." That voice was magical. It should have belonged to an angel or a devil, not a man. It would have lulled him somewhat, if he'd let it. "It is time to go back now."

"I know," Tryton sighed. "I know it is."

"We need you."

"Yes." Everything went gray.

And the sea was gone from him again.

* * * * *

"I began to think I would never find you."

"I was not ready to be found," Tryton said frankly.

"I am sorry."

Tryton looked at his most trusted friend and ally, The Traveler, also known as Grimm the Wanderer, Grimm the Invincible, Grimm the Legendary and — more recently — The Grimm Reaper or Reaper Man. He looked as calm and controlled as ever, but there was something more to him now. An urgency crawling just below the surface that no one would notice, unless they knew him as well as Tryton did.

"I know you are truly sorry, and I thank you for it," Tryton nodded solemnly. "What has happened?"

"Much. And there is much that *will* happen, or so I am warned."

"Tell me what you can." Tryton leaned back into the deep cushions of his chair and stared deep into the flickering flames of the fire that burned in the hearth of the great stone fireplace in his public sitting room. He could still smell the salt on his skin, feel the warmth of the sun radiating from his body…he did his best to ignore it.

"Cady and Obsidian were attacked on a recent visit to the surface world, by yet another new and very powerful breed of Daemon. They were almost killed."

"But they have recovered?"

"Not through any effort on our part, but yes they are well."

Everything was forgotten—the sea, the sun, the earth's fresh air—as Tryton felt a cold shaft of foreboding race down his back. Every hair on his body rose with foreboding. "Whose efforts saved them then, if not ours?"

"Two men. Strangers by all accounts. They appeared on the battlefield after Obsidian had been—" he hesitated, as if unsure. And Grimm was never unsure. Tryton frowned, willing him to continue. "After Obsidian had been killed, and Cady was nearly ready to follow him into death. They revived Obsidian and healed our Cady. But that is not all."

Tryton closed his eyes and took a deep breath. He feared he already knew what would come next.

"One of the men had your face. According to Cady, the similarities were so striking, he could have in fact *been* you. I'm not entirely certain she's ruling out the possibility that it was you."

Tryton shuddered. "Damn."

"I cannot track them, I have already tried. They are cunning, and it appears they do not wish to be found."

"Two of them?"

"Yes." Grimm stood so still he could have been made of stone.

"What did the other look like?"

"We don't know. Cady says he's Shikar, or like us enough to have our eyes."

All Shikar shared the same eyes, except for the more experienced members of the Traveler Caste. Travelers like Grimm. Spending too much time wandering between worlds seemed to change them somehow, both their spirit and their eyes—the very windows to the soul. Grimm's eyes were black as death, but tiny pinpoints of light shone here and there like glittering stars. Grimm's eyes had been like that for centuries now, but Tryton could remember a time when they had been filled with the same golden fire that burned in his own eyes.

Those days had been much happier ones. Tryton wished now that he had held on to them longer, cherished them and reveled in them for as long as he could. But alas…it had been he, himself who had changed that simple happiness into struggle and worry. Everything that had gone wrong, all of it, was his fault and there was nothing he could do now but regret it.

"This is unexpected," Tryton murmured. "*Two* of them."

"That is not the only reason I've searched for you. I have had a vision."

This too-bland statement surprised Tryton into forgetting for the moment the worry of the strange man who looked like him. "About all of this, about Obsidian and Cady?"

"No. About something else." Grimm paced again, clearly full of barely restrained energy. "Raine came to me in a dream. And she came with a warning."

"Raine again," Tryton frowned, wondering. "What can the Shade of a human woman have to do with any of this—with any of us?"

"She was Steffy's friend and Emily's sister. Perhaps she still feels those ties, even in death," Grimm offered. It was an old discussion between them by now.

"I think it is more." Tryton studied him closely, then broached the subject that had been on both their minds, thought neither had spoken of it. "She is dead, my friend. You cannot be with her. A love between you is impossible."

"I know that." Grimm's voice was so quiet, so soft, that Tryton had to strain to hear it.

Tryton let the sensitive issue rest, but he knew it would continue to plague them both. Grimm was in far too deep with the ghost of Raine already, the heartache had only just begun. "What was her warning?" Tryton urged his friend onward.

"The Horde is stirring again, despite our last battle which should have decimated their numbers. The Daemons that attacked Cady and Obsidian were incredibly strong, unexpectedly so. I do not think their leader is letting go of this fight, I think he is making new, even more powerful monsters. And now he is unleashing them. Raine told me they are moving to capture a human woman, in less than a few hours from now. I wasted precious hours to find you, but Raine told me you were necessary to save this woman, to prevent her capture."

"They mean to *capture* her?" he started. "You're sure?"

Grimm nodded, his hair shining like blood in the light. "Just as they intended to capture Emily, before she mated with Edge."

"But why capture them? In all these years, the Daemons have only fed on humans. Why would they need to take them alive? What purpose could that serve?"

"Perhaps Lord Daemon has some nefarious plans for the women," Grimm mused aloud, "though how that might endanger us or help his army, I couldn't say. I've never understood his mad reasoning."

"But if he means to continue this fight, why did he go missing for so long? Why come back now after withdrawing his power from the Daemons? And why did he sa—"

"Tryton!" Cady, the first human-turned-Shikar, raced into the room. She skidded to a halt, eyes wide with surprise—and not a little wariness, given that the last time she'd seen his face her husband had been dead and she had been close to the same fate. "My god, *you're so dark*! And your hair is so blonde it looks *white*. What in the hell have you been doing all this time, buying out QVC's self-tanners?"

Tryton let the words he'd been speaking to Grimm die away. He smiled at the small, curvaceous woman whom he considered a great and dear friend and tried not to think of the dark days that surely lay ahead. "Cady, my dear, you look radiant."

"She carries my babe again," Obsidian, Cady's Shikar Warrior husband, proudly announced as he joined them. "So of course she would look thus."

"That is indeed good news," Tryton exclaimed, rising to envelop Cady in a warm, heartfelt embrace. "Congratulations."

"You didn't answer my question," Cady pressed stubbornly, suspiciously, even as she heartily returned

Tryton's hug. "Where have you been and what have you been doing?"

"Will the others be arriving soon? We have precious little time to spare," Grimm interrupted their reunion with that eerie, dead calm that was uniquely his.

"We're here." Edge strode into the room, his wife Emily at his side. Directly behind followed Steffy and Cinder. The entire team — Tryton's team of seemingly invincible warriors — was assembled.

"We haven't much time, so I'll be brief. There's much I need to tell you. Much I've kept from you for far too long. But something — someone — has forced my hand and now you must all know the whole of the truth. Firstly we have a mission and we cannot fail or it will be disastrous," Tryton informed them hurriedly.

"What must we do?" Obsidian, ever the fierce warrior, cut straight to the heart of the matter with no preamble.

"There is a human woman in danger of being hunted and captured by the Daemons — "

"Niki Akitoye," Emily whispered at once.

Tryton nodded solemnly. "Your sister's Shade told you as well, I see."

Grimm said nothing, merely looking into the flames of the fire in the hearth as if all the answers to their questions could be found within the flickering depths. If he was surprised or disappointed that Raine had felt the need to visit someone else besides him, he didn't show it.

"We have to find her," Emily said simply.

"And we will," Tryton said, the wealth of confidence in his voice more for their morale than his own. He had had long years of practice in keeping all of his worries and doubts to himself. "As soon as The Traveler tells us *where* to find her."

Grimm raised his head, black eyes sweeping over everyone in the room. He slowly adjusted his cloak, raising the hooded cowl to hide his features. "She'll be at the Seattle airport. But we have to hurry or we'll miss her getting off the plane."

"There is no way the Daemons could attack in such a public place," Edge interjected.

"Are you sure that's where Raine told you to find her?" Tryton asked Grimm, managing to keep his own skepticism from showing in his voice—but only barely.

"Raine told me that Niki would be crossing the Mississippi. But I..." he faltered, but only long enough for Tryton to notice the telltale hesitation. "I just know that she is headed for Seattle. I cannot explain it. I just know it."

"I do too," Emily offered immediately. "I think Raine might have told us that somehow, without her having to say it. You're right, Grimm, we have to go to the Seattle airport—we can't just pop in on the plane en route to get her, after all."

"You are right, that would be impossible. Let us join hands everyone," Tryton commanded. "We will all wait for her in Seattle."

"You're going with us?" Cinder asked with no small amount of surprise.

"He has to," Emily murmured with a perplexed frown and puzzled eyes, as if wondering how she also knew that bit of information.

"For whatever purpose, Raine thinks I should go. And so I will. She has yet to steer us wrong and I can do no less than to trust her in this." But Tryton wished it otherwise. It was dangerous for him to venture out into the open field of battle like this—like a red flag waving before an enraged bull, the Daemons would sense him, and they would be moved to take action.

But when had he not lived in constant danger? If not from the Daemons, then from the discovery of his own people. No matter how many things changed over the centuries, one thing still remained the same.

He could not escape this conflict.

No matter how hard he tried, it was inevitable that it eventually end.

Grimm reached out. They all joined hands and prepared to Travel. To meet their destiny together.

"Wait! Wait!" A breathless Desondra—one of the Shikar females, wife to a brave and well-respected warrior named Zim, and aunt to Cinder—burst into the room at a sprint. "There's been something horrible," she gasped for breath, "something absolutely terrible has happened— wait!"

"Holy fuck," Steffy shuddered. Tryton eyed her, knowing her precognitive abilities—even stronger now that she was a Shikar instead of a mere human—gave her an edge like no other. Without being told further he knew this did not bode well, for them or for the mysterious Niki Akitoye.

Steffy's eyes burned into his as she met his gaze, as if she'd known he'd be looking back at her expectantly. He felt his heart plummet.

"We're already too late," she whispered.

Chapter Three

She knew her eyes were open and yet she could not see.

The last thing Niki remembered was the turbulence. Not too strange a thing, given that she'd been soaring thirty thousand feet in the air and yet...it had been such a clear day, no clouds or rain showers in sight around or below the airplane. And the shaking and shimmying had been enough to trip the flight attendants in the aisles. Maybe it *had* been a little strange after all.

What had happened? Had they crashed? Was she dead? Was that why she couldn't see anything, did souls even need sight in the afterlife?

A sharp pain in her head as she shook it made her realize she was still alive after all. What a gyp it would be if one could still feel pain in the afterlife! No, she was still living. But if she wasn't dead, what had happened and where was she exactly?

It was so dark here. Wherever *here* was.

Searching around her on hands and knees, she tried to gain some hold over the situation she found herself in. The ground beneath her was cold and hard, slimy like wet cave rock. She made her way only a few feet, it couldn't have been any more than that, when she bumped headfirst into a wall. With a curse at the unexpected obstacle she stood and felt her way up the wall, all the while straining to see something, anything, in the impenetrable dark.

The wall veered inward sharply and her hands reached for empty space. It hadn't been a wall after all, but an enormous boulder or shelf of rock. And even without seeing or feeling her way further, she knew something horrible was waiting just beyond the slab.

Stop. You don't want to know any of what lies beyond this rock, a stranger's voice—a husky female voice—warned in her head. *In fact you don't want to hang around here at all. Get out now while you can.*

But she couldn't see to find her way out. It was just too black, with no light to guide her.

Get going and fuck the light. If you don't leave now, find some way out of here, you'll never see the light again.

Niki couldn't waste any more time worrying about the darkness, not after hearing the stark power of warning in that voice ringing through her aching head. With the loss of sight, she had to rely heavily on her other remaining senses. The cold felt like the handle of the cellar door of the house she'd grown up in as a child.

She realized that she was underground.

The smell of the dank was the smell of the Earth gone wet and stagnant and cool. But beneath that smell was the faintest scent of sun-warmed sand, a slight perfume she might never have noticed had she not been concentrating so hard on each detail of her surroundings.

Turning away from the horrifying enigma of the stone boulder, she followed that scent in the hopes that it would carry her away from the grave omen of mortal danger that permeated this place. Despite the darkness, she hurried, feeling a strange crawling sensation at the base of her neck, as if something terrible were dogging her every step.

For a chilling moment she feared that if she looked behind her now, she would be able to see all too clearly that which had been invisible but scant moments ago.

Niki experienced a monstrous, overwhelming fear unlike any other she'd ever felt before...and despite the blinding dark, she began to run as fast as her shaking legs could carry her.

* * * * *

"The plane stalled in midair and crashed in a field in Kansas."

"How would you know all this, Desondra?" Cinder asked his aunt, not a small amount of suspicion lacing his tone.

Desondra swiftly darted her golden eyes in Tryton's direction.

"That is one of the many things I must discuss with you upon our return," he told the group.

Desondra's dusky bronze skin paled alarmingly.

Cady noticed this but ignored it, for she already knew Desondra's secret—as did the other women in the room. Instead, she zeroed in on what Tryton had just said.

"What do you mean 'upon our return'? Our return from where? What's the point in us leaving for Seattle when the woman is already dead?"

"She isn't dead," Steffy interjected.

All eyes turned to her.

Steffy's face was as silvery pale as the blonde roots that peeked out beneath her short, spiky purple hair. "The Daemons took her. That's why the plane crashed, that's why we have to go—we have to find her."

"But go where?" Cady growled, impatient as always to have all the facts laid out as soon as possible. She hated not knowing what they might be in for, damn Tryton and his enigmatic ways. Damn Steffy for being precognitive and just as secretive about it. And damn Sid for being so calm in all of this chaos. She almost swatted his rump in her frustration.

Steffy took a deep breath, then released it, sounding just as frustrated as Cady. "I don't know."

"Yes you do," Tryton said calmly. "You just need to concentrate. Think of where we might find this Niki Akitoye. If there is any one among us who can lead us to her, it is you, and we are counting upon it."

"Raine didn't tell us she would be taken in midair," Emily bit out. "Why wouldn't she have warned us of that?"

"Perhaps she didn't foresee it. She is but a Shade after all. She is not all powerful," Tryton suggested.

Grimm's jaw tightened at the reminder that Raine, however helpful she might be, was still dead. Still an outsider. Still so far out of his and everyone else's reach.

Steffy ignored all of this and went to sit down in Tryton's chair before the great, roaring fireplace. There was always a flame, always warmth here. She let it lull her. Let it calm her as she watched the hypnotic dance of the flickering fire light.

Where was Niki Akitoye? Where could they find her? And how could they save her—

"I know where she is," Steffy said, hearing the wonder in her voice as she realized that she did indeed know exactly where to look for Niki. "Oh my god, it worked."

Tryton smiled knowingly at her. He'd always been the one with the most faith in her precognitive abilities. She felt a sudden wash of pride that she'd been able to help them in this small way. That she might yet be able to help save the missing woman who was in so much grave danger.

"Where must we go?" Edge spoke at last, ever the most serious one in the group. Always ready to fulfill his duty, whatever, wherever it may be.

"Egypt," Steffy said with a smile, rising from the chair.

"Egypt!" came the collective gasp from many in the room.

Tryton and Grimm remained conspicuously silent.

"Yes," Steffy continued. "The Giza complex if you want me to be precise. I think she'll be crawling out of a hole about a mile west from the Great Sphinx, near a dilapidated parking lot, in but a few short minutes. And we really have to hurry," she frowned, feeling an altogether new urgency take her. "Something is chasing her."

Grimm came forth, arms outstretched, and they all gathered around him. Touching him, holding onto some piece of him, ensured that they would all Travel safely with him. An instant trip across the miles and dimensions, safe in the cocoon of Grimm's enormous power. In but a second they would all be in Egypt, awaiting Niki Akitoye and whatever was rushing after her, ready to fight to the death to protect the strange woman none of them had even met yet.

All because Raine had willed it so.

* * * * *

Niki's arms and legs pumped in time with her racing heartbeat as she sprinted to get as far away from her unseen pursuer as she could. How long she'd been running was a mystery to her, but her sides and lungs ached with a sharp and blinding fire unlike any pain she'd ever experienced before. It had been a long time, was all she knew for certain.

And still she ran.

She knew without having to see, that whatever gained behind her was not something she wanted to have to face, no matter the cost. She had to escape it. Her life depended upon it.

Bright spots danced before her eyes and she wondered briefly if she might pass out or expire from a heart attack in mid-run.

Bright spots—wait! She could *see* again! Only barely. But enough to know that somewhere up ahead there was a light. Silvery and faint, it called to her and she followed. Finding some secret store of energy locked deep within her, she ran even faster, ignoring her pain and weakness and fatigue as hope soared within her breast.

Not far now. Yes, she could see it, up ahead. A sliver of moonlight. The scent of warm sand was greater now, and growing stronger with each running step she took. Less than a quarter of a mile up ahead she would find salvation from the darkness.

Her heart nearly stopped beating as the thing behind her let out a great, bellowing roar of rage.

If she'd had enough breath to spare, she would have screamed. This was the first real proof that something was indeed chasing after her. Up until now she might have been able, later on, to chalk it up to paranoia. But it seemed her instinctive panic had helped to get her moving fast enough to save her life, because whatever was after her, it sounded really pissed that it hadn't caught her yet.

The roar came again, louder this time, closer.

Niki's breath whistled in her burning lips, stretching the flesh of her seared lungs like helium rushing into a balloon. She'd heard that sound before, long before now...oh sweet god, how she'd prayed for so long never to hear it again.

It was one of *them*. One of those ghastly creatures she'd tried so desperately to convince herself were just figments of her overstressed imagination. It was a monster, right out of her past, only this time she knew for certain it was real and not a hallucination.

Damn fate. Damn life. She wished she'd died long before this moment, in ignorance and relative bliss, without this affirmation that these abominable things did indeed exist.

Anger rose in her breast, usurping the primal fear. Fury, the likes of which mortally alarmed her, boiled in her blood. For years she'd been avoiding the burn of rage, the rush of anger or even aggravation. Horrible, terrible things happened when she became angry. People died. Lives changed forever in but the blink of an eye. It was why she was so cautious, so careful in everything she did. She must never lose control.

But maybe this time, of all times, her anger would serve her far better than her caution.

God, she hoped she wouldn't have to put it to the test. Impossibly she strained to run faster, ever faster, towards the sliver of pale light just up ahead.

When at last she reached the source of the illumination, she almost screamed in sudden frustration. The beacon of light was small—too small—peering through but a small hole in the ceiling of the strange, earthen tunnel. But she couldn't give up, couldn't let this setback deter her, for surely the monster at her heels was but seconds away from snatching her up in its clawing grasp.

She had to get out. Now.

Niki could just fit her hand through a crack in the stone. With a jerk and a grunt, she pulled at that opening, and a rain of dust and earth showered upon her. The hole was wider now and her hopes soared. Desperately, she punched at it and more earth fell away. A waterfall of sand followed, coating her from head to feet, smelling like the salvation of open air and warmth. Her laugh of triumph sounded mad even in her own ears.

Another roar, this one almost on top of her now, and she gritted her teeth for one last desperate attempt to widen the hole just enough for her to climb through and escape to freedom beyond it. She struck at the opening, jerked and pulled at the overhead crevasse in growing panic and frustration. Rocks and sand and debris stung her hands until they bled and throbbed and swelled.

And finally, at last, a massive chunk of cement or stone or something really heavy, fell down at her feet— barely missing her head, though at the moment she wasn't sure if that was a lucky thing or not, considering her pursuer was so close she could smell its fetid stench. Bright, silvery moonlight streamed in, bathing her in a halo of illumination. She giggled, though it sounded more like a growl, and scrambled to climb her way up and out.

When she was free, she collapsed on her side upon the sandy ground, shaking. The warmth of fresh air had never felt or tasted so deliciously sweet.

"Get up, Niki, you're not out of the woods yet," she warned herself unsteadily, testing her voice around giant gulps of air.

But her body was so tired. Running full out again seemed beyond her now.

With what last little strength she possessed, she crawled to her hands and knees, scurrying away from the hole behind her, uncaring what direction she headed in — so long as it was away from that *thing* following her.

Niki had made it no more than a few dozen feet when the ground exploded upward behind her and she knew, at last, after all the struggle and pain, she was well and truly caught.

The past five years had all been spent in solitude and in caution for nothing.

Chapter Four

Tryton looked around the moment the world rematerialized again. Indeed they were in Egypt, a place he'd never thought to visit again. It held far too many painful memories for him...

But everything, it seemed, was coming full circle at last. Millennia after millennia had passed over the world, but still there was no escaping fate, not even after such a vast stretch of eons. Not for humans, not for Shikars. And especially, certainly, not for him. A full reckoning was due and had been for a very long time. And perhaps, after all, he had not yet paid his debt in full.

A shudder quaked the earth, drawing his eyes to the source of the disturbance.

A Daemon ruptured a chasm in the ground, its body erupting from it like a wash of pure evil. The creature, at first glance, was one not so different from any Tryton had seen in the past, but another look showed that perhaps in small ways it was. This one seemed more humanoid than any other he'd previously encountered. Its skin was still bubbly, slimy and scaly at the same time, black and brown like sewer sludge and undoubtedly smelling just as foul. Its teeth were tusks in its mouth, but the face still held the lips, the nose and the forehead of a human. It possessed anatomically correct arms and legs, fingers and toes...it was a grotesque caricature of a Homo erectus. Not quite yet a Homo sapiens, though, thank all the gods that ever were.

Lord Daemon had grown so powerful that he was finally drawing closer to the secret of golem resurrection, it seemed. It was only a matter of time now...and time, unfortunately, was something the Lord of the Horde had in spades.

Just as Tryton did.

Indeed, all the secrets Tryton had kept over the years were way overdue in sharing with his team.

Damn it. He hadn't wanted things to be this way.

Desperate to gain some focal point in the chaos, he roved his eyes over the destruction of the ground, the angry Daemon, and the surrounding area, looking for the woman. Looking for Niki Akitoye.

What he saw stole his breath away, but for entirely unexpected reasons, ones that he would never have guessed if given the chance, which he wasn't.

Niki Akitoye was a goddess from the past, a woman unlike any he'd seen since the dawn of the golden age of Egypt. A creation of such perfection that she could, and no doubt did, make the heavens weep with envy.

His heart sped up, racing madly in his chest in a way he'd never before experienced in all his endless years.

He was frozen in place. For the first time he knew what it was like to be paralyzed by emotion. And by all the power of all the worlds combined, he craved more of these feelings.

But first, he must save the goddess from the beast that stalked her.

All of this had happened within a few short seconds, but to him it had seemed an eternity. If time could stop, he would have sworn it did for him with his first glimpse of Niki Akitoye. Even sprawled on the ground, crawling crablike away from her attacker, all her dark chocolate skin scraped, bruised and exposed by her cutoff jean shorts and sleeveless top, she was the most glorious thing he'd even laid eyes on.

The Daemon roared as it prepared to launch itself at its prey.

Tryton's team of warriors moved as one to intercept the monster's charge.

Tryton raised his hands, drawing desperately upon his full power to call the water from the beast and turn its form to dust in its tracks.

But something happened. And none of the all-powerful could do anything to stop it.

Niki roared back suddenly, stunning them all into motionless silence. She gained her feet in a neat little somersaulting move and faced her attacker. An intense wave of heat that had nothing to do with the desert air — for it was night and cool as the desert could get — washed over them all.

Power, pure and exquisite, invaded Tryton's pores, but it was not his own. His senses expanded and he knew — he felt — that his comrades in arms felt exactly the same wash of supernatural force as he did. His cock hardened. His heart swelled full to bursting. And on the wind he smelled the warm musk of jasmine and vanilla. Such a delicious perfume, it made him want the woman with a crazed lust that nearly drove him mad.

A jealous, burning, possessive rage made him wonder if the others — especially the men — felt this intense lust. He wouldn't have it. He would not allow it. Niki was not for them. This lust was to be his and his alone or he'd kill every last man who looked at her, no matter the cost to his soul or honor.

The power flooded him again, taking away all rational—and irrational—thought.

It was coming from Niki, this magic. The tidal wave of energy, fed and fueled by her rage and overwhelming emotion, had turned them all to stone, unable to move, it seemed.

The Daemon dropped to the ground, mewling and screaming. It bucked in pain. Twitched a few times. And then went still.

"No fucking way," Cady whispered in shock.

"*Scheiße*," Steffy echoed.

"What the hell just happened?" both Edge and Cinder growled in unison.

"How did she do that?" Emily asked dazedly.

"I don't know," Obsidian's deep voice sounded calmer than the others, but only just. "But I intend to find out."

Grimm, it seemed, was content as ever to hold his own council.

Tryton was beyond words. He'd never seen anything like this, never felt anything like the overwhelming flow of strength and magic that had lashed out from the woman like a tidal wave. It was incredible, it was shocking.

He wanted to feel it again.

With long, determined strides, he approached the woman, who stood still as a soapstone carving, eyes wide with a storm of emotions he couldn't read or understand. He didn't know exactly what he planned to do, didn't know if he would scare her or if she would merely throw her incredible power out to him in an effort to protect herself, and he didn't care. All he knew was that he had to be near her. Had to touch her. Had to feel the warmth and softness of her tender human skin, and know that she was real and not fantasy.

She didn't seem to notice him—though her eyes remained wide, they were unseeing, shocked. He caught her up in his arms, holding her so tight he knew he would leave faint bruises upon her flesh. Her scent, her sensual, earthy perfume of jasmine and vanilla, drowned his senses. He fisted a hand in her long, riotous black curls and made her look at him.

At last her eyes met his. He felt he might drown in the endless depths of those dark, brown orbs.

"I claim you, woman," he heard himself say, as if from miles off. "You're mine now."

He slanted his mouth over hers and Traveled them instantly home, uncaring of the shocked, amazed stares of the comrades he left behind. Nothing mattered but that he get this woman, Niki—his Niki—safe within his lair as soon as possible.

Fate, it seemed, was not without an ironic sense of humor. And damned if he was able to prevent any of this from happening, though he knew it would all end in chaos. The reckoning would come and there was nothing he could have done to prevent it. Niki was in his arms, her mouth sweet and shocked and open beneath his. He wanted her. Fate had won and he would not fight it.

It was already far too late for that anyway. It had been the moment he laid eyes on her.

* * * * *

"What the hell just happened?" Emily exploded as Tryton and Niki disappeared.

"Did I actually see that?" Cinder sputtered.

"He kissed her," Steffy smiled.

"Does he know her from somewhere else, maybe?" Cady frowned.

"No," Grimm murmured. "But it seems that will not stop The Elder from claiming what he wants when he finds it."

"Oh boy, here we go again. Only it's the matchmaker's turn," Cady laughed.

"I do not think it will be so simple this time," Grimm warned.

"Simple. You call mine and Sid's mating simple? Shit, a more complicated match there never was—except for Steffy and Cinder's. And Edge and Emily's. Only this time, at least, we know the woman is gifted. We know she can become one of us. Tryton had no such knowledge when he first pushed me and Sid together."

"We shall see."

"Quit being so doomsday-ish Grimm," Steffy grinned. "Let's just sit back and see what happens shall we?"

"Yeah. But first, let's go over and check out this Daemon. I want to make certain it's dead and assure myself that there are no more of them before we go back home." Emily stalked over to the fallen monster's form.

"She didn't take the heart," Cady warned. It was well-known that to truly kill the beast, the heart—the seeming source of its life force—must be destroyed.

"She didn't have to," Grimm said softly at their backs.

"She stopped it," Steffy marveled, kicking the side of the corpse, "with her mind. She killed it without even having to touch it."

"Impossible," Edge gritted out, a long silver-blue foil shooting from one finger. He used the blade to slice open the monster's chest cavity.

The heart within was shriveled up, like a raisin. Lifeless and defeated, it did not beat.

"Holy shit!" Cinder exclaimed.

Steffy froze, her breath escaping her in a rush that startled nearly everyone around her.

Grimm remained stoically silent, as if he already knew what she had found, and perhaps he did know. He was The Traveler, after all. He seemed to know everything.

Steffy bent, dug delicately into the squishy ooze of the Daemon's flesh. With an unpleasant, sucking sound, she freed something, grasping it tightly in her fist.

"*Scheiße, Scheiße, Scheiße,*" she echoed over and over, words so fast they nearly tripped over one another. A stream of German hummed through her lips, and the Shikar—all master linguists at birth—could barely follow her.

Steffy at last tore her wide gaze away from the odd, tarnished object in her hand, casting her eyes to Cinder in silent supplication.

"That's an officer's badge," Emily, a former police officer herself, instantly recognized it.

"Oh no," Cinder took the slimy badge from Steffy's shaking fingers. "How can this be possible?"

"I've seen this badge before," Steffy's voice sounded choked and swamped with her fear and disbelief.

"Where?" Cady immediately demanded, grabbing for the badge to take a look for herself, as if the answer might lie there, but Cinder held fast and would not release it.

Cinder and Steffy regarded each other for a long, silent moment, while everyone else waited with baited breath for them to explain their reaction to the badge.

"Officer Ehlers..." Steffy swallowed hard. "He was there when we were attacked by Daemons that night, when Cinder and I were in Germany."

"The night Cinder burned that field down with his firebomb," Cady remembered the tale. Cinder had stunned them all. They had known he was a powerful Incinerator, but *that* powerful...it had boggled the mind. He had decimated a Horde Canker-Worm, and an entire field of crops besides. It was an incredible testament to his Caste strength and warrior prowess.

"Yes. But I never saw Officer Ehlers get killed. He had disappeared..."

"The Daemon must have killed him and taken his badge—for whatever reason. I've never claimed to understand how—or even if—these monsters think," Edge growled.

Cinder turned back to the Daemon. He squatted down beside it, poked and prodded at it for several moments. Steffy knelt down beside him and reached for something in the muck.

It was a scrap of very stained, very rotted piece of cloth. It might have once been an odd pea-green color, or even blue, there was no real way to know.

But Steffy knew. She instinctively cast her eyes up towards Grimm, who stood calm and still in the shadows.

"This is a piece of Ehlers' uniform," Steffy's tone seemed to accuse him.

But Grimm held his secrets, just as well or better perhaps, than Tryton did.

"Ask The Elder your questions upon our return, if you wish to obtain answers," his words confirmed to them all that he knew those answers but would not share them.

"Why the fuck does a Daemon have a police officer's badge and part of his uniform?" Emily roared at him.

Grimm held his silence.

"I'm getting sick and tired of all this secrecy shit between you and Tryton and us," Cady growled.

Grimm's eyes glittered like stars beneath the black cowl that covered his face. "I do not give a damn, Cady," he said flatly. "Ask Tryton your questions if you must, the answers are not mine to give."

Cady stomped towards him, anger emanating from her in waves. A halo of fire danced around her hair. She, too, was an Incinerator—like Cinder—and it clearly showed now with her volatile storm of emotions.

"Do not anger me, little Cady," Grimm warned. For the first time in a very, very long time, each and every Shikar there remembered why he had been so feared and so revered all these years.

Ten thousand years had passed since Grimm had made his mark as one of the greatest warriors the Shikar race had ever known. But sometimes, the passage of time could dim a memory...Grimm seemed more than capable of keeping that memory alive. He was dangerous— perhaps the most dangerous being alive but for Tryton— and he reminded them all of that now with his tone and with his words.

Grimm sighed suddenly, further surprising them all. "I do not wish to intimidate you, really I do not. But I ask that you respect my vows of secrecy. I repeat, ask The Elder your questions. Tryton is ready now, I think, to give you the information you have sought for so many generations."

"I have a feeling we won't like hearing what he has to tell us," said Cinder.

"You won't," Grimm promised darkly.

"Let's go home," Cady said with a shaking voice, still eyeing Grimm—a man who she regarded as a great friend and ally—warily. She'd never heard him speak with such dangerous power in his voice as when he'd warned her not to anger him. She felt like she didn't know him, as if he were a stranger, though how could that be?

She'd known him for years. She and Sid had made love for his viewing pleasure countless times. She'd seen the man naked—shockingly, gloriously naked—so many times, the image was burned on her brain. And yet she had never truly sensed the vast scope of his awesome strength and presence before tonight.

It scared the shit out of her, this seemingly abrupt shift in Grimm's demeanor.

And from the wary looks on all her friends' faces as they moved closer to Grimm for the Traveling, she knew it scared the shit out of them as well.

Things, it seemed, were about to change. The rules of the game, the war itself, had shifted inexplicably. Unexpectedly. And she was damned if she knew how, after Tryton told them all the secrets they wanted to know, things could ever be the same in their world again.

Chapter Five

Somehow they'd ended up here, in this strange, mammoth stone chamber, and she had no memory of *how* they'd arrived.

Her mind was a whirlwind of confused emotions.

Niki felt the hard, hot slant of the golden Adonis' mouth over hers. Shock—both from the long, hard run and from the climactic death of the monster—made her slow in responding, but respond she did. How could she not have?

He was the most amazingly gorgeous man she'd ever clapped eyes on.

But there was something more. Something incredible and terrifying in the way that he held her, so tight and possessive in his arms. Something in the way he kissed her that let her know he was so much more than just a man, gorgeous or otherwise.

His tongue was a hot flame dancing in her mouth, stroking her teeth and laving the roof of her mouth. Tasting her more deeply than any lover ever had dared before. As if he wanted to eat her alive. As if he wanted to swallow her whole.

The wide, flat press of his palm against her bottom, drawing her hips harder into the cradle of his, made her heart race. His fingers were so long, his palms so broad. She felt dwarfed, and she was not small by any means. He was so tall, so strong, so incredibly *big* that he was overwhelming.

Her nipples felt like burning stars on her swollen, heaving breasts. She couldn't resist rubbing them against the rippling thrust of muscles on his chest and nearly swooned with the sensations as she did so. The man's mouth pressed and moved over hers and the kiss consumed her whole world. Her mouth was filled with the spicy, manly taste of him. Her nose filled with the scent of rain and tangy ocean air.

The enormous jut of his cock against her, rubbing against the crest of her sex and belly, brought her out of her fugue and she remembered herself at last.

Bracing her hands against his shockingly broad shoulders she pushed with all of her might, but he would not release her from his embrace. Indeed, he didn't even seem to notice her struggles. She pushed again and tried to turn her face away from his sinfully skilled lips. Those lips followed her, never once parting from the kiss.

Despite that he was a stranger, despite that she felt sure she might be in some very real danger with this man, she felt herself grow weak and wet with desire.

The man must has sensed this too, for he growled low in his throat—a sound that vibrated into her mouth and lungs along with the warmth and flavor of his breath— and ground his hips harder against hers.

God, he was so big. All of him. Huge, even!

Niki realized her eyes were closed and forced them open. With a shock that could have melted her very bones, she met the golden-orange glow of his awaiting gaze. Now she knew why people closed their eyes when they kissed—it was far too intimate, far too intense to stare into each other's eyes this way. It was as if they were looking deep into each other's souls and there was nowhere, no way to hide.

Niki shoved again, using the last of her strength to prove—if not to him, then to herself—that she was trying her very best to put a stop to this before it was too late.

The man growled again and loosened his hold on her. But he did not by any means set her free. Instead, he sucked her lower lip into his mouth, licking and drawing on it until she was completely lightheaded with arousal. One of his hands was still fisted in her hair, holding her captive in an almost primitive way. The other rubbed and squeezed the plump globes of her ass.

Thunder racketed the air around them.

Her heart fluttered. Her breasts ached. Her insides clenched with a force that would have stolen her breath if his kiss hadn't already. Wet and swollen with need, she let her lips relax beneath his once more. She opened her mouth wide for his tongue again, and could have died with ecstasy when he gave it to her.

Had she ever wanted this much, so quickly?

Was this all a dream? A nightmare of monsters turned to a delicious wet dream with a totally, inconceivably sensual sex god? Did it really matter?

Niki heard a moan and was mortified to realize it was she who had made the urgent, husky sound. She hadn't known until now that she could even make such a sound. Until this moment, she hadn't known so many things about herself.

Was it safe to learn any more?

"Let me go." She found the strength to gasp the words into his mouth.

He growled again but made no further response, merely ran his tongue along the length of hers, deep into the hot cave of her mouth as if she'd never spoken.

"I said," she pushed hard, with all her might, "*let me go.*" She jerked her mouth away, feeling like a fool when he followed her and made her move it again and again, until she was shaking her head back and forth with desperate violence.

She kicked him in the shin.

His fingers dug deeper into the cheeks of her bottom to hold her still.

She bit at his seeking lips.

He wrenched her head back with the hand still fisted in her hair and laved the vulnerable expanse of her throat with his tongue.

Panic swamped her. Would this man ever release her, or would he continue to take and take until she was limp and weak in his arms? Her heart sped up, her head felt light, her vision dimmed.

Oh *no*.

The warmth of her magic filled her veins until they burned. Damn it. She didn't want to hurt him. He needed to let her go *now*.

Power swelled between them, she could almost see it. Almost taste it.

"Stop, stop," she begged.

His hips ground into hers.

Her hands began to shake and she beat them desperately about his shoulders.

It was too late. She felt the strange, unearthly wrenching as the storm of her strange magic erupted from her and struck out at him. For the second time that night she knew someone would die—but this time the target of her overwhelming power was not a beast but a man.

She cried out. Too late.

She could not contain it, the magic was unleashed. The man clenched her tighter to him—both arms around her—threw back his head and let out a mighty roar. His body shook against hers, taking the full brute force of her uncontrollable psychic attack.

Damn him, why hadn't he released her? Why hadn't he listened?

Not another one, please, don't let this be another death on my conscience.

The man jerked against her, nearly crushing her bones in his ever-tightening grip, then sank to his knees before her. Niki felt her heart nearly shatter. *She'd killed him.*

The man gave a final moan and buried his face into the soft mound of her belly, both hands clenching her hips tight with desperation. While Niki had feared the stranger's embrace, while she had sought release from his too-wicked kiss, she hadn't wanted it to end this way. This was yet another death on her hands, which were already stained dark with blood…

"Forgive me," the man rasped against her.

Niki started. He had the strength to speak these last words and he'd asked *her* for forgiveness?

"I'm so sorry," she whimpered.

"I've never been so careless before," he continued, astonishing her.

He didn't sound at all near death. He sounded...languorous. Replete. As if they'd just made love.

How completely unexpected.

"Are you all right?" she asked hesitantly, dreading and fearing his answer. Her head ached from expending so much psychic energy.

His eyes rose up to meet hers again, glowing bright with a preternatural orange flame. "I've never felt better." Desire, thick and heady and quite intimidating in its intensity, coated each word.

He sighed and buried his face back into her belly, nuzzling her. "I've never come so hard before. You've driven me mad."

Niki frowned.

The bastard! He'd not been struck down by her power after all, he'd only creamed himself! She jerked away from him and this time he could not hold her to him, he was still too enthralled in the aftermath of his pleasure.

Niki moved to put the distance of the room between them, putting her back firmly against an earthen wall, hoping its support could keep her shaking legs from buckling. Their eyes met and locked. No matter how she might try, she could not pull her gaze away from his as he knelt there, recovering, in the middle of the great room.

"What the hell just happened?" She finally found her voice after several tries. "Am I dreaming or what? One minute I'm in an airplane and the next—god damn—tell me I'm dreaming, *please*."

"You are Niki Akitoye?" His eyes never left hers. They were so bright, so vividly colored, she felt hypnotized by them.

"This isn't happening." She stubbornly refused to answer him. Her head was pounding and she winced with the pain.

"I am Tryton." He rose slowly to his feet.

Damn, but the man was tall. Nearly seven feet if he was an inch. With shoulders as broad as a barn and muscles that would have made an Olympic bodybuilder weep with envy. He carried his size so well, his every move completely controlled and full of grace, and Niki felt something low inside of her clench with lust.

Her eyes drank him in from head to toe. He had the longest, softest looking hair—so blond as to be nearly white in some places. The bright, unearthly eyes were slanted almost like a cat's. The irises were wide and bold around large black pupils, rimmed with tones of gold and orange around a band of red fire. His skin was a deep, dark bronze, contrasting starkly with his pale hair and glowing eyes.

He was dressed in worn jeans and a black t-shirt, but for some reason the clothes looked all wrong on him. Too normal. Too human. And the faint stain at his crotch, a growing patch of dampness, definitely made her uncomfortable.

"What are you?" The words trembled on her lips.

"Do not be afraid, my goddess," he soothed.

Her womb positively throbbed with need at the sound of his voice, so low and soft and coaxing.

"I mean you no harm," he continued. "I am Tryton, of the Shikar Alliance. I swear to you that I shall protect you from the Daemons who hunt you. You have no need to fear anymore."

"Daemons?"

"The monster you killed is from a race of abominations we call Daemons. We were warned that you were in danger from them and charged with the responsibility of saving you from them—"

"This isn't happening." She took deep, panting breaths. Her vision was blurry, her head hurting worse and worse with each pounding beat of her heart.

Instantly he was at her side, stroking his hand over her hair in what he must have thought was a soothing manner.

It wasn't. Niki shrieked and jerked away from him, relieved when he did not follow. "Don't touch me!"

"I won't hurt you, woman."

She bristled at his show of affronted dignity. How dare he address her as "woman"! She liked "my goddess" better. "Just stay away, alright?"

He nodded his head, eyes solemn. "As you wish."

"This isn't a dream," she blinked, hard.

"No." His voice was so sexy, she couldn't think straight. "It isn't."

"The plane crashed," she shuddered. Her stomach roiled as the pain in her head threatened to swallow her skull.

"Yes, but you were not in it at the time. You were taken by the Daemons in mid-flight, an unexpected event. We did not think they would risk so much just to capture you. There were many witnesses to your abduction, an unfortunate circumstance, but not wholly damning for the Alliance. The particulars of the event are already known by your news media, but luckily for us, humans rarely believe such fantastical tales and the story will be glossed over heavily. The secrecy of the Daemons' existence will be maintained. Few will believe the truth and the people who watched the Daemons take you will eventually tell themselves it was all a bizarre mass hallucination, the result of injuries they might have sustained in the crash. Eventually, they will *believe* their own lies."

His words weren't making much sense to her, though his tone suggested he was trying to calm her. Like that would be possible after the night she'd just had. Oh god! She'd almost forgotten! "Jada is waiting for me at the airport. She'll be looking for me. I have to go to her before she hears about the crash—"

"You have no more ties to your world or the people in it. You are under our protection now. I cannot allow you to leave. Let this Jada person concern you no more, in time she will be only a dim memory."

Anger flared and along with it a new wave of pain. "Jada is my *daughter*, you son of a bitch, and I'm on my way to get her whether you allow it or not!"

But she wasn't going anywhere and she knew it. Not for the moment at least…

The look of wide-eyed surprise on his face was the last thing she saw before the pain took her in a rush and she fell gasping to the floor.

* * * * *

Tryton tenderly cradled Niki's head in his lap. He knew he should probably settle her on his bed, where she would be more comfortable when she roused from her faint, but he couldn't bring himself to move just yet. It was far too sweet to hold her like this as she rested, limp in his embrace.

A *daughter*? This beautiful, exquisite goddess was a mother? How incredible. While this somewhat complicated his goals of seducing her, it warmed his heart in a totally unexpected, surprisingly tender way.

A child. Could he, the ancient and all-powerful Shikar Elder, actually assume the role of father when the time came?

And he fully intended for that time to come.

He wanted Niki Akitoye. The very second he'd laid eyes on her he'd known that he was forever lost to her and no other. She was sheer perfection in all ways. A woman like no other in all the world. He wanted her sex. Wanted her heart. He wanted her very soul. And to know that she had a child of her womb…it made her all the more ripe, all the more sensual in his eyes. There was nothing sexier than a woman who was also a mother.

And how old was this child? Was she young enough for Tryton to lavish all the best trinkets and affection upon? Or was she older, closer to adulthood, someone to whom Tryton could provide funds for schooling, material adult comforts and the like? Was she as beautiful as her mother—would he have to fend off her overzealous suitors like any good, loving father should? This was such an unexpected blessing—he hardly knew what to think.

He was perhaps getting a little ahead of himself. He knew that. But yet…they had never felt so right, these protective, nurturing instincts swelling within him now, no matter that in this case they were a bit premature. He wanted Niki Akitoye, and nothing less than her all would do. He wanted everything. And if she had children, then he wanted them too and all the responsibilities that came with them.

The soft, thick mass of her black curls felt like warm, living silk in his hands. He couldn't seem to tear his hands away from it. But it was also a torture. His cock had never been so hard. His body had never been so fevered, so assaulted by pure, scalding hot lust.

He wanted to make love to her. No. He wanted to fuck her. To bury his cock to the heart of her until she screamed her orgasm to the heavens as he brought her over and over again to release. He wanted to go at her for hours, stroking in and out of her wet heat a thousand times before finding his own release. He wanted her limp and nearly unconscious in his arms, completely undone by the pleasure he knew for certain only he could give her.

More than once he'd mated with a human woman until she was senseless, completely mindless for days. And those women had been veritable strangers, pretty faces that meant nothing to him. It would be so different, so much better with Niki, for she had already inspired more feeling in his dead heart than any other before her.

Though he was incapable of love—he'd known this unavoidable truth for eons now—he was not incapable of tender feelings. He felt sure that he could keep Niki happy and well-satisfied in his bed and in his life. She would never want for anything and it wouldn't matter that he could not truly, fully love her.

He would accept no less than her total surrender and her total happiness.

With a primitive hunger he'd never experienced before, he drank in every nuance of her face and form. She was so close to perfect that it nearly hurt to look upon her. She was quite tall for her sex and for her species. Though he still felt her fragility like a warning in his brain, and though he felt so much like a giant when he stood over her, it turned him on mightily to know that he would be able to take her standing up with only a little effort and adjustment.

The lushness of her curves was incredibly feminine. Large breasts, soft, rounded belly, and wide hips that would cushion even his most powerful thrusts made him think of nothing but sex, sex and more sex. Her skin was so dark as to be completely black—not brown, not beige, but pure ebony darkness that made his mouth water and his fingers itch to touch all the satiny softness of her.

There was ancient beauty and grace in her proud countenance. Her high forehead, stubbornly rounded nose, lush, full lips and almond-shaped eyes blatantly attested to her Nubian heritage. It made him remember long ago days spent in the open, lush greenery of the Nile river valley long before it had all turned to so much dust. Even her scent, spicy and exotic, brought back flashes of memory, of times spent in the villages and temples of the ancient peoples of Egypt.

Her hair fascinated him. His gaze and his need always went back to her hair. It was long and thick and riotously curly. Black as midnight and surprisingly silky, he could not help but wrap its length around and around his wrists, as if to imprison her in the most elemental way possible. He wanted to fist his hands in her hair, hold her head as far back as it would go and sink his cock into the depths of her mouth and throat until she swallowed him whole.

He shifted uncomfortably beneath her. His phallus was so hard, so engorged, that it actually pushed her head up in his lap. He'd orgasmed earlier and the dampness was growing more than a little uncomfortable against his swelling flesh. He needed to control his urges, at least until he knew that this woman and her daughter were safe. He needed to slow down or he would surely devour her whole and scare her to madness in the doing.

But he'd never been so tempted, so close to losing control. Nor had he ever been so close to the edge of sheer, sexual madness. Where was his normal caution? What had happened to his cool, calm, mentor's exterior?

It had vanished, lost in the glory of her face and form—and all that was left in its wake was hungry, demanding male.

Tryton gritted his teeth against the painful swelling of his cock and rose with her in his arms. Effortlessly bearing her weight, he carried her from the room, on into his sleeping chamber, and laid her down gently upon the massive bed situated in the middle of the room. There was no power in existence that could have prevented him from running his hand down the side of her neck, across her breasts, onto her belly and down one of her long, long legs. He fisted his hand, savoring the feel of her, and turned away.

He needed to get out of these human clothes fast. They were simply not built for the massive endowments of a Shikar male. The jeans bit at him, confining his erection until he felt more pain than arousal. The worn cotton shirt stretched and pulled over his wide chest and arms, no matter how he pulled and tugged at it for more room. It had been so long since he'd worn such human bonds that he had forgotten just how *different* the human anatomy could be. It had been even longer since he'd felt the stirrings of desire when caught in such confines.

Unbuttoning the clasp of his pants he nearly groaned with relief. His erection sprang free, heavy, long and thick, it bobbed before him. He sighed heavily and wiped at the residue of his release with the hem of his shirt. Clearly, jeans and t-shirts were never meant to house the form of a fully aroused Shikar warrior. He hurried to remove the rest of his soiled garments.

* * * * *

Niki opened her eyes a slit to see what he was up to.

Holy hell…he was *up* to a lot.

The last lingering traces of her headache swiftly receded in the face of such a surprising—hell, *alarming*—sight. The man, Tryton, was naked and moving about the room, uncaring or unaware that she had a full view of him in all his natural glory.

Wow.

Niki had never been a shy virgin, not in her whole life, and she was proud of it. She reveled in her sensuality whenever she got the chance, which lately wasn't quite often enough. She'd had many lovers in her time, men of all races and color. In fact, the father of her child Jada had been a lovely, white-skinned man…unfortunately he'd turned out to be a complete bastard, but still, he'd been beautiful. Incredible in bed, even if he'd been a jerk out of it. Simply put, his body had been amazing—the best ever.

She had never, *ever*, seen a man quite so amazing as this…Tryton.

God, his dick must be at least a foot long! It was wide, thick and heavy as it bounced up and down with each step he took. No matter how many men she'd found pleasure with, she remembered clearly that none of them had been that well endowed.

Damn, his legs were long. Not only were they long, they were heavy with the same bulging muscle that covered the rest of him. He was completely hairless—

maybe he waxed, though he didn't seem the type to be vain enough for that—except for that glorious length of platinum blond hair that swung freely down to his ass.

And that ass...she licked her lips appreciatively. Toned and firm it was, perfection like nothing she'd ever seen. A runway model, fitness guru, or upscale gigolo would kill for that bum, no question. Her fingers clenched with the need to squeeze those sculpted globes...she remembered a phrase she'd once heard on television and nearly laughed. *His ass was so perky you could have bounced a quarter off of it.* Whoever had come up with that line must have been imagining this man and no other.

God he was *hot*.

Not only that, but he'd kissed her, which meant there was no reason why she should just sit here and let all that dark, bronzed, muscled flesh of his go to waste.

She almost called out to him before she remembered. Everything.

"Get dressed, Adonis," she growled, sitting up in the bed, "and take me to my daughter."

Chapter Six

Tryton knew the moment she awakened. Knew the second her gaze had locked onto his body—he'd felt it roving all over him like a thousand caresses across his hot, fevered skin.

He'd been looking for a robe to don, something comfortable that might hide his need for her when the others arrived, as he knew they inevitably would. But as soon as he'd felt her gaze eating him up, he'd felt less like protecting her from the sight of him and more like teasing her with the inevitable reality of what would be between them when she finally let him have his way.

It had pleased him mightily to hear the muffled beat of her heart quicken, along with her unsteady breaths. Oh, he definitely had an effect on her, and no matter how hard she might try to hide that from him in the days ahead— she undoubtedly would, she was only human after all— her body could never lie to him. Her body wanted him and it was only a matter of time before her mind would want him too. After that...

She would belong to him. Completely. He would see to it.

Parading in front of her like this was making him even more desperate for her. A mischievous streak he'd not even known he possessed made him reach to palm himself. How would she react if he began to pleasure himself, right here, in front of her? But before he could test it, she spoke, effectively breaking the sinfully erotic spell that had woven about them both.

"Get dressed, Adonis, and take me to my daughter."

For a moment he doubted his hearing. Had she, a puny human woman, dared to order him about? And in his own domain no less. He, the great and mighty Tryton, The Elder of the Shikar people, followed no orders. He was a law unto himself and had been for thousands upon thousands of years. How dare she presume to take such a tone with him?

Perhaps he had heard her wrong. All the arousal and need had flooded his brain...surely he'd heard wrong.

"I beg your pardon," he said softly, warningly, knowing she would not be rash or bold enough to command him again.

Her eyes widened. She was no fool, she'd heard the danger lurking beneath his quiet words. He nearly smiled, knowing she would apologize now for her impertinence.

Then she scowled, surprising him yet again. "You heard me. I said get dressed and take me to my daughter." She folded her arms over her chest and glared at him.

The woman must be daft after her faint. No one had ever dared speak to him thus.

He decided to be gentle with her, at least until she regained her self-control. Moving to a large, ornate wardrobe — intricately carved and decorated by Edge, who was a master craftsman with wood — he flung the doors open and reached for the closest article of clothing within. A soft pair of dark, earthen brown trousers would provide ample room for his endowments. The loose, flowing material might not do much to hide anything, but it would at least be comfortable. And comfort he would need if he was to spend any more time with this she-devil of sensuality.

His chest he left bare, just to spite her.

The front of the trousers laced up with a supple leather tie and he turned to her as he worked the laces over his erection, knowing she watched his every move with more than a little interest. He wanted her to see the effect she had on him now, wanted to perhaps intimidate her as well as titillate. Once the cloth was securely fastened over him, he stroked himself, settling his heavy tumescence with unnecessary showmanship.

He was more than pleased when he saw the wet tip of her tender, pink tongue dart out over her lips.

He wanted that tongue to dart out over his cock, and vowed to himself that it would happen very, very soon.

They looked at each other, guarded and aroused and not a little agitated.

"Take me to Jada," she repeated.

"No." He felt one corner of his mouth tilt up in a half smile.

Her eyes flared upon seeing it. "Yes," she barked, rising from the bed, volatile in her indignation.

"You will not leave here, you are in far too much danger. I will send someone for her and have her brought here," he explained patiently.

"Are you stupid, she won't go anywhere with a stranger! She's probably already heard about the crash—I need to get to her as soon as possible! Where are we anyway?" She looked about as if the answer lay waiting for her in the impenetrable stone walls. "How long will it take us to get to her?"

Tryton sighed. His desire for her was making him daft. He knew a mother's love was stronger than any other, and he knew also that the girl Jada must be in as much danger as her mother. If the Daemons got to her first…

He left the room and approached the great fireplace in his meeting chamber. He grabbed a fistful of fl'shan sand from an urn on the mantle and tossed it into the fire, which immediately roared to violent life.

"Come to me, my Travelers," he murmured in the ancient tongue of his ancestors. The fl'shan sand, an old forgotten magic only just rediscovered, would work as a vehicle in the fire to call out to Grimm and Emily, to grab their attention no matter where they were or what they were doing, and compel them to come at once.

He heard Niki stomp into the room. And felt Grimm appear, silent as the grave, at his side, followed a millisecond later by Emily.

Niki barely managed to muffle a shriek of surprise, and he couldn't help grinning. If Niki was surprised by this…well, she hadn't seen anything yet.

Niki knew he was gloating, damn the man. But hell, she'd just seen two people appear out of thin air! Though she was no stranger to the paranormal herself, she was by no means used to seeing other people perform such feats right before her eyes as if they were as commonplace as a sneeze.

"Niki, this is Grimm and Emily. They will go in your place to find your daughter and bring her back safely."

Emily, a small woman with striking black hair and a peaches and cream complexion, visibly started. "You have a daughter?" she asked.

"Why are you all so damn surprised at the mention of a daughter?" Niki exploded, feeling more and more like an oddity in their midst. Who were these people anyway? Better yet, *what* were they? "Yes, I have a daughter. She's waiting on me at the airport right now and if I don't show up soon she'll think I'm dead in that crash—"

"We will find her," the tall man in the black cloak—Grimm—told her calmly.

"Do you maybe have a picture of her on you?" Emily asked, moving closer.

It was only when the woman stopped about three feet in front of her that Niki noticed the color of her eyes. Or the lack of color...Emily's eyes were completely black! With some effort, Niki answered the woman's question.

"I'm afraid I didn't remember a purse."

"There is no need for sarcasm." Emily smiled a little as she said it.

"We've no need of a picture either." Grimm came towards her too, but he did not stop as Emily had. He reached out and took Niki's head in his hands, gently enough, but when she tried to pull away—his touch and his presence were too overwhelming, too intimidating—he held her still. "Let me see her," he whispered for her ears alone and she stilled, entranced.

There was such *power* in that voice...she had to obey him. The feel of the cool skin of his hands against her temples made her shudder, but not entirely from fear. He was too much, this Grimm. Too much of everything. Power, might, sensuality, danger, and cold-blooded calculation, he was all of that and more.

A second and it was over, but in her mind his touch had lasted an eternity. Her head ached for a moment, that old familiar pain from too much psychic exertion, and then eased.

"A young one, no longer a child but not yet a woman," Grimm murmured. "We will find her."

"Let Emily approach her," Tryton warned. "You might frighten her away."

Emily grinned. "No shit."

And with that, the two disappeared without a trace.

It took a good minute to recover, but she managed, despite Tryton's heavy stare. "What the hell just happened here?" Niki demanded.

"They are my Travelers. My couriers, if you will, at least in this case. They will find your Jada for you."

"But how will they know where to look? How will they find her?"

Tryton smiled, revealing a dazzling set of perfect, white teeth. Her gut clenched tightly and her heart raced. God, he was gorgeous.

"Grimm learned all he needed from you. Don't worry, Jada will be found and kept safe from harm."

"What is happening here?" She felt a wave of worry and panic. "Who are you people and what do you want with me?" She put her hands to her head, exactly where Grimm had put his before, as if she could squeeze the answers out herself. "I didn't do anything to deserve this. I just wanted to help people—I just wanted to help her, and what do I get for it? Powers I can't understand and nightmares that will last me the rest of my life. Damn it, it's all *her* fault!"

"Whose fault?" He frowned. "Jada's? I don't understand."

It was just too much, all of it. Niki growled and shook her fists at him. "No! This—all of this—the healing, the headaches, the nightmares, the monsters, the deaths, all this is because of that woman!" She growled and stomped her foot, giving vent to the impotent rage she'd never before allowed herself to truly, fully feel. "If it weren't for her driving in that goddamn blizzard, none of this would have ever happened, none of it. If I hadn't been on duty that night I never would have been there. But I was and I tried—*oh, I really tried*—to save her. But I couldn't. I just couldn't.

"Now I've got these powers, I can do the most amazing and the most horrible things. There have been so many times when I've almost lost it completely. I had to send my daughter away to a boarding school just to keep her safe—if I lose control, I might kill her as I did the others. I have to move all the time so people won't discover my secret. I can't hold a normal job, I can't have a home—I can't have a relationship with anyone! I'm tired of the headaches, tired of the magic and the nightmares, all of it. I just want things back to the way they were before that night...damn it," she finished on a hoarse whisper.

Tryton eyed her strangely, something serious and calculating in his eyes that hadn't been there before, and it alarmed her.

"I'm sorry," she said with a shudder. "I've never exploded like that before. I don't really feel sorry for myself and don't normally complain or pitch fits like that. It was uncalled for and you didn't deserve to witness it. It's just," she faltered. "I just feel like..." She couldn't find the words.

"You feel out of control," he offered.

Yes, she did. But she wouldn't admit it to him.

"Tell me more. How is it that you gained these powers, this magic of yours, if you were not born with them?"

Niki shook her head, ashamed that she'd been so loose with her emotions in front of this stranger, unwilling to share more. She started when he jerked her chin up with his fingers — she hadn't seen or heard him approach.

"Look at me," he commanded.

How could she not? He was holding her captive with his bright, glowing eyes as easily as he did with the fingers holding her chin in a gentle vise.

"Tell me everything," he said softly, too softly.

She wanted to say no. She wanted to refuse him. She didn't know him from Adam and wanted nothing further to do with him. But to her complete, utter surprise, she told him everything he wanted to know. For the first time she told him what she had not told another living soul, not even her daughter. And heaven help her, she held nothing back.

* * * * *

"There she is."

Emily looked over the sea of people to see for herself. "She's not at all how I would have pictured her," was all she could manage.

"You should make the first move," Grimm instructed quietly.

He stayed in the background as she walked forward to do just that. The girl — more a young woman than a child — watched her every step as though, despite the crowd, she knew that Emily was coming toward her specifically. Jada was her name, or so Grimm had told her in the endless moments it had taken for them to arrive here.

Despite what everyone thought, Traveling took a long, long time. At least it seemed that way to the Traveler doing it. Emily hadn't understood just how Traveling worked until after her shift from human to Shikar, when she'd awakened as one of the Traveling Caste. Now she felt she knew far too much about it, despite the fact that she was still "in training".

Travelers, contrary to popular belief, did not just disappear and reappear at will. No. It was far more complicated than that. Travelers were the vehicles by which others could disappear and reappear at will. Unlike other Castes, Travelers had the ability to fold space and dimension. But it was not at all easy, and when "folding", time became skewed. It passed by very, very slowly.

What might seem like a two-second trip to a non-Traveler, to Emily felt more like several hours. When she was in that state of in-between, Traveling from one space and time to another, she was moving over incredible distances. And with each trip, she felt the toll of those distances weighing heavier and heavier upon her.

She knew now why Grimm was so still and so silent. He existed apart from everyone else. There was no one who was not a fellow Caste member who could understand the immense weight resting upon his shoulders. He was truly alone. Now she, too, was much the same, though her husband Edge kept her from getting lost in that lonely place of unbelonging. Grimm, however, had no one. And he'd had no one for several thousand years. Emily could not imagine so desolate an existence, growing greater and greater each and every time Grimm Traveled for his beloved Shikars.

There would come a day, she knew, when she grew too tired to go on. It was then that she would leave to that far-off place of nothingness, to die or to live forever as only a spirit or vapor...she wasn't sure. But that's what Travelers did — they simply left. Never to return.

Edge vowed she would not go into that place alone. He promised that he would join her in that dim and long-off future. And for that she was eternally grateful.

Grimm however, would go alone. For the woman he loved — everyone by now must know he loved her sister, Raine — was dead and gone from him. Far beyond even his long reach. There would be no ever after with a heart's love for him. There would be only emptiness — and an eternity of it at that.

Looking at Niki's daughter now, something about Jada reminded Emily of just such a vast emptiness. An aura or air about her that proclaimed her lonesome existence within this sea of unconcerned, preoccupied strangers.

"Where is my mother?" the girl asked without preamble.

Emily tried not to fall into the depths of the girl's deep brown eyes. She felt certain that if she looked too hard there, she would drown. "She's waiting for you. My name is Emily and I'm a friend of hers, will you come with me?"

Jada rolled her eyes. "Mom has no friends. Tell me what she looks like, then I'll come with you. Maybe."

It was hard to hold back her grin, but somehow Emily managed. The girl was so serious, Emily knew better than to make light of her caution. "She's tall, with long, curly black hair, dark eyes like yours, ebony complexion, pointed chin, long-fingered hands. Oh," she'd almost forgotten, and a good police officer—which she'd been in a former life—never forgot the important details. "And she has a scar on the back of her right knee from when she was burning brush in the backyard when you were seven and an ember caught her."

"I was eight," Jada said smartly, but her smile was easy and accepting. "How'd you know about that? Mom doesn't tell anybody about that—she's embarrassed by it. She hates being clumsy."

Emily smiled. Niki certainly hadn't told her, but Grimm had, and Grimm had a way of knowing all the right things at all the right times. "Are those your bags?" She motioned towards the two duffle bags piled haphazardly on the seat behind Jada.

"Yeah." Jada picked them up now, slinging one over each shoulder, brushing aside Emily's offer of aid. "I heard there was a plane crash and I was afraid it was Mom's."

"Didn't you know what flight she was on?"

"No," Jada snorted, looking far older than her thirteen years should allow. "Really, I wasn't sure when Mom would get here, but I knew she would come. She always comes when I break out of school."

Emily nearly choked on her surprise. "Break out of school? What do you mean?"

Jada's large, dark eyes rolled again. It was a look fast becoming something Emily expected from her. "Break out, escape, run away, does that spell it out for you? I left in the middle of the day, the dean called her in a panic because she couldn't find me, and Mom knew I'd be here waiting for her. We've done this several times before—hasn't she told you that? No, she's probably ashamed of that, too. Hell, she's ashamed to even come here to get me this time.

But what does she expect? This is the only way I get to visit with her. My 'acting out' as everyone likes to call it, is probably just a cry for her attention or whatever, yeah, but it's *her* attention I want. This way I get to spend a few weeks with her while she tries to find another boarding school that will take me, and I've got a record for truancy now so that's getting harder and harder to do. Shit, maybe this time she'll give up and send me to a normal school with all the normal kids so I can go back to living with her."

"That was a lot of words for someone so small, and I don't think you should be swearing," Emily said sternly. "It's not ladylike."

Jada plopped one of her bags on the ground unceremoniously and eyed her. "Are you telling me that you don't swear? Because I won't believe it—I *know* things, and I know you swear."

Emily didn't know what to say to that. "Come on," she said at last, snatching up the fallen bag herself before Jada could. "Your mom did want to come," she led the way to Grimm, who stood out like a sore thumb in the crowd with his dark robes and towering height. "She just couldn't make it."

"Where is she then? Are you taking me to Savannah, is she still living there? Or are we going to Biloxi, or Tallahassee or any of the other cities she's lived in for the past five years?"

They came to a halt next to Grimm.

"Holy crap," Jada said, looking up, up, and up into Grimm's cowl. "Are you a basketball player?" she asked bluntly.

"No," he answered.

"Why's your face covered?"

He ignored her and turned to Emily. "Are you prepared? We must time this perfectly."

Emily nodded, it was best to be at their most careful now. They appeared in the airport at the best moment to avoid detection and they must leave in the same manner. It would not do at all to have people see them simply disappear as if by magic.

"Fine, don't talk to me then," Jada snapped at him. She turned as if to leave them. "Tell Mom I'll be waiting here for her to come fetch me herself."

"Girl," Grimm reached out to snag a handful of material at Jada's shoulder.

For the first time, Emily got a clear glimpse of Grimm in an unguarded moment. Indeed he appeared almost flustered around the girl. She wondered, with a sense of awe, if he'd ever really interacted with human children before, for indeed it seemed that he had not.

Jada swatted at his hands, unafraid and belligerent as a thirteen-year-old could be. "I'll scream and say you tried to snatch me," she threatened. "The security around here is tight as hell. I doubt you'd have time to get away."

Grimm growled—he actually growled—and reached for Jada's hand. A second later—at least for the girl—they were underground, in the world of the Shikar, in the living room of Emily's apartment.

"Neat," Jada said, looking around, as comfortable now as she'd been in the airport, as if she'd Traveled a thousand times before. "Now what?"

"Now I'm getting out of here," Grimm said hurriedly and disappeared.

"Boys," Jada said trenchantly, rolling her eyes again. "They're so totally chicken."

Emily only smiled.

"So, wanna tell me what's going on?" Jada smiled back, with an all too knowing, all too mischievous glint in her eyes. "'Cause that was no ordinary plane ride we just took."

"Well *duh*," Emily said with a smile.

Chapter Seven

Tryton watched over her as she slept, for the second time that night. Niki's face was streaked and marred by tears, but even so, it was more beautiful to him now than it had been even a few hours before.

How had things come full circle like this? Was it fate? Was it chance? Or was it on purpose, all of it, some as yet undiscovered machination that he simply hadn't even suspected all this time?

He hated surprises. Such surprises shouldn't even be possible to one as old and jaded as he, but there it was, staring him in the face — the hidden connection, the truth, the reality of it all.

How could he not have known?

How could he not have seen?

Niki had told him everything and yet she had no idea just how explosive her tale had been to him. To the Shikar Alliance as a whole. It was astounding.

She had told him. She had wept. His mind and his soul had wept with her. And when she finished she had slept, as if the revelation of her secrets — even to one who was as yet a stranger to her — was a burden that had sapped her of all remaining strength. Niki slept deeply now, dreamless — he'd seen to that personally with but a light touch upon her mind — and he was loathe to wake her. But wake her he must, for time was not in their favor and rest would soon prove a luxury for them all.

There was so much to do and the window of opportunity in which to see it all done right was closing fast.

He nudged her gently, and called her name until she stirred. Gods, she was beautiful, soft and dazed with sleep and exhaustion. It took all his control not to reach out and take what he wanted.

It was the second time she'd awakened to find herself in his bed, and she was fast becoming used to such a wicked comfort. As she fully roused, Niki's vision was filled with the overwhelming sight of his exposed torso. Dark and bronze—a true golden-bronze hue—he looked like a wet dream come to warm and breathing life. For those first few moments between sleep and wakefulness, she forgot all her worries, all her sins. Nothing concerned her but him. And she made the decision that would, inevitably, change both their lives.

"Kiss me," she whispered, reaching for him.

His eyes flared wide with surprise. But he willingly came to her embrace, bending his leonine head and pressing his hot, hard mouth to hers.

Desire flared instantly to life within her. A need and a yearning so great, it made all others before it pale in comparison. It felt as though perhaps even her most explosive orgasm in the past had been but a dim shadow, a mere preparation for this moment, this kiss, this man.

His hand smoothed her hair away from her face and neck, coming to rest pressed against her throat in a purely dominant way that had her heart performing somersaults within her breast. He held her jaw in his powerful fingers, turning her this way and that as their kiss deepened into a thoroughly passionate exploration.

The feel of his tongue undid her. It was burning hot, textured velvet as it brushed and tangled hers, as it danced and laved over her lips. He kept flicking it against the corner of her mouth, as if he couldn't help himself. It was such an erotic, earthy, male caress — that flicking of his tongue — that it made her head spin out of control.

The tips of his fingers kept kneading her jaw, reminding her that he was the master of their embrace, no matter that she had instigated it. Heat emanated off his bared chest in suffocating waves. Her hands *had* to touch, *had* to feel and grasp at that gorgeous skin.

She pressed her palms flat against the large, rounded mass of his pecs. His nipples were tiny, hard nubs beneath her fingertips. She rolled them gently between her fingers and he moved against her like a surge of the sea.

He definitely liked that.

He parted her lips wider with his, pressing harder against her until her mouth was completely open and gasping beneath his kiss. He was devouring her, ruthless and completely demanding. There was nothing she could do to protect herself, and if there had been, would she have wanted to?

Oh, he tasted like sin. Like rock-hard man and dangerous predator. Utterly primal and completely unpredictable. His tongue flicked the corner of her mouth again, and then once more, wringing a moan from the depths of her. He kissed like a man on death row. But, too, he kissed like a man who was used to spending a small eternity in bed with a woman.

Her hands swept up his body, over his — oh damn, they were so wide! — shoulders, and further, to reach around his neck. His hair was so long. Thick and silky and completely, gut-wrenchingly, sexy. She'd never felt hair so soft before. It seemed unfair that it should belong to a man.

There was so much heat, touching him was like touching the sun. But the burn of him only made her burn *for* him all the more.

When one of his hands moved to cup her breast, she nearly screamed with excitement. As if he had all the time and patience in the world, he held her there for long, endless moments. Then, slowly—so achingly, arrogantly slowly—he flicked his fingers over the straining erection of her nipple.

She bucked beneath him, gasping into the moist hot depths of his mouth. His tongue swept over her upper lip, as if to praise her—or punish her—for her response. Everything he did drove her wild. Wilder. She was going insane with lust!

He was practically lying beside her on the bed now. Lounging like a god with the world but a toy in his hands, he seemed completely in control of the situation, whereas she was a puddle of sheer excitement.

"Feel something," she rasped into his kiss.

"I feel." He flicked his tongue against the corner of her mouth again.

She turned into him—they were both on their sides now—and he never once let her lips free. His hand plumped and squeezed her breast as she arched into him. He turned, taking her with him, the hand at her throat and chin moving to tangle fiercely in the hair at her nape. His other hand moved down and around to cup and squeeze her buttocks, and then she was lying fully on top of him.

The bass rumble of thunder echoed about the room and Niki wondered if it was the sound of her heart pounding in her ears.

He arched his hips into hers, at the same time pulling her down with the hand on her ass, so that there could be no doubt just how *much* he felt the effects of their embrace. The loose, soft fabric of his trousers hid nothing from her…*thank god*.

"I feel," he murmured softly, patiently. "I feel you."

She melted onto him, like a pool of honey fresh and warm from the hive. He pulled her head down to his, and rejoined their kiss as if she'd never interrupted it. His hand toyed with the waistband of her jeans before slipping beneath it and beyond. She was wearing a thong and there was nothing to shield her skin from his palm and fingertips. He hooked one of those fingers in the strap of lace that lined the crevice of her bottom and tugged gently upon it.

He was using her panties to caress her from anus to clit. The feel of the delicate lace rubbing against her with each tug of his finger had her whimpering helplessly. He swallowed each sound she made, lapping them up with his tongue to savor them as his due. Each tug of his finger grew stronger, each of her gasps more desperate, and she wondered crazily if she could come this way.

No. He would not let her. Just as she teetered, preparing to step off that sheer cliff into oblivion, he eased her, stroked her from nape to thigh as if she were a pet.

She growled, frustrated beyond any boundary she'd crossed before.

His tongue flicked the corners of her mouth.

She bit at him, angry that he would and could deny her such pleasure so easily and not seem fazed by it at all.

He jerked her head back by the hair and pressed a hard, rough kiss to the vulnerable arch of her throat. When she would have protested, Tryton rolled her beneath him, taking her down deep into the mattress with his weight, and sucked her skin into his mouth, marking her.

Niki hooked her hands over the immense bulge of the muscles of his arms as they caged her. She pulled ineffectively, not even knowing what she was struggling against anymore. He rocked his hips into hers rhythmically, rubbing his erection against the ultra-sensitive core of her until she subsided and began to move with him.

It was like a dance. Withdraw, advance, withdraw. Over and over his body moved into hers, rubbing, stroking, rocking. Like the calm, endless motions of the sea, he was the god of the ocean that swept her up into passion's depths. The tempo set between them was the beating of his heart, the slow, steady draw of his breath.

Her heart was thundering. Her lungs were shuddering, panting for air as if she were running a race and couldn't get enough oxygen.

When he began kissing a path down her throat, she almost fainted. He caught the material of her shirt in his hands and to her complete and utter shock he ripped it down the middle, rending it from her completely with brutal efficiency. Her bra followed in much the same fashion. The soft hiss of tearing silk excited her far more than she could handle and she almost climaxed just from that sound alone.

And the feel of his mouth...she did scream when he touched her then. So hot, so wet, so tight, he drew her nipple into his mouth like a hedonist might draw upon a piece of fruit fed to him by the fingers of a lover. Her hands tangled in the softness of his hair, fisting and clenching with each deep pull of his lips.

His hips rotated in erotic circles against her. His teeth pinched her nipple, just a point beyond gentleness, and she cried out mindlessly. Her ankles crossed in the dip of his back, her arms held his head to her breast like a babe. His hands roved over every inch of her, teasing and titillating until she could have sworn that he had not two, but two thousand hands.

It felt like forever that he played there at her nipple before he moved further down to her belly. His hands worked the fastening of her jeans, pushing them down—his first real show of impatience—until she was clad only in her white lace thong. The flame of his tongue rimmed her navel, each exhalation of his breath warming and tickling her flesh.

"No more waiting," he said, as if to himself more than to her, but nevertheless his words enflamed her further.

Tryton jerked back, rearing over her, pushing her knees up to her chest and spreading them wide. He jerked the material of her thong aside, ripping it and casting it away. She was finally fully exposed to his gaze and he took every advantage of that. His eyes drank her up, roving over her from head to toe, leaving no part of her unexplored. The wet, swollen pink lips of her cunt seemed to fascinate him, drawing his gaze again and again until he seemed unable to look away.

She'd never been more vulnerable. So fully opened and aroused.

Tryton held her effortlessly with but one powerful hand, while the other moved to unlace the ties of his pants. At that moment, Niki saw their shaking, their unsteady motions and gave a sigh. He was *affected*! All that iron self-control had been nothing but a show, a ruse. She would have shouted her triumph and elation to the heavens if what he revealed then hadn't stolen her breath away completely.

No way. *No way* was that going to fit inside of her.

The thick, long swell of his cock was bigger now—oh shit, it was so much bigger!—than it had been when she'd glimpsed it earlier. She jerked back, an elemental and instinctive panic gripping her.

"No." He held her tight, moving to cover her. "No you don't, not now that we've come this far," he rumbled.

His gaze locked with hers and would not set her free. She was trapped by his body and his eyes and there was nothing she could do about it. He sank into her. His body was so hot, so hard, so masculine. She could have wept.

She did weep, a little, when his cock began to stretch her. From pain or from pleasure she wasn't sure and knew it didn't matter. If he stopped now she'd surely die. He wouldn't let her arch up beneath him, wouldn't let her move to hasten their joining at all. Niki cried out, feeling the burn of him as each inch impaled her more deeply, more tightly, more fully.

God, he was so long. So thick and so hard. But he moved slowly into her, letting her body grow used to his invasion. While she might appreciate this thoughtfulness of his later—much later—for now all she wanted was to be fucked and fucked raw.

"Please," she begged over and over, thrashing her head about on the pillows.

His gaze would not let go of hers. She felt afraid suddenly, not of his sex and not of his passion, but of his sheer intensity. Could he see into the depths of her soul with those bright, flaming eyes? Had she no secrets from him, no defenses?

"I own you now," he breathed, licking her mouth erotically, still coming into her.

Oh god. She spasmed around him and he slid home at last, deep into the heart of her, to the very mouth of her womb.

"Your body is mine." He touched her breasts. "These are mine." He moved his hand lower to her belly. "This curve, this softness is mine." He moved it down further, taking the swollen bead of her clit between his thumb and forefinger, stroking it mercilessly. "This pussy is mine. All of you, everything you are, is mine. *My* goddess, *my* woman."

"No." She could not look away from his eyes.

"Yes, yes, and yes a thousand times." He pressed his lips to hers again and again. His fingers stroked her clit in wide, firm circles. His tongue invaded her mouth and withdrew and with it, his body withdrew, leaving her bereft. She moaned. His tongue filled her again, as did his cock. Again. And again. And again.

She was panting, moaning, arching beneath him.

He was licking, stroking, and thrusting into her.

All the while their gazes remained locked, wide open, missing nothing.

His pupils flared, until nearly all of the shocking yellow fire was gone. The press and stroke of his fingers over her clit drove her up, only to soothe her when she approached too closely to release, easing her back down only to start all over again. His thrusts took her deep, until she was nearly sobbing with the need for relief. He was stretching her channel, filling her until she felt like nothing more than a quivering mass of nerve endings that screamed with the need for his touch.

"Oh, oh, oh," she panted into his mouth.

His thrusts echoed her every sound, her every breath.

"I need it," she begged.

"What do you need?" he urged, biting gently on the end of her chin.

"Let me," she cried.

"Let you what?" He was merciless.

She beat his shoulders, hating his control. "You're making me crazy."

"I went crazy the first moment I saw you," he said, watching her intently.

It was upon her and neither of them could stop it, even if they had tried. He pushed deep into her one last time, his gaze never leaving her face, his fingers massaging her clit to milk it from her, and she was flying.

She screamed, she cried, she choked on the sea of ecstasy that threatened to drown her. Her body shuddered beneath his, her pussy milking his cock like a fist until she was sobbing, it was just too much. Her ears roared, her heart galloped. Tremors rocked her from head to toe, centering in her lips and breasts, down to her belly and pussy. It was the most powerful thing she'd ever experienced.

And when she came down, several minutes later, he was waiting for her.

"No," she begged. It was too much.

"Yes." He shifted her, bringing her ankles around his back.

"Please."

"I know, baby," he soothed, thrusting his body in and out of her again.

"I can't."

"You can." He angled his thrusts to rub against her clit, to stroke against her G-spot. "You will."

She shuddered. He sucked her breast into his mouth as far as he could manage, drawing brutally upon her until she was gasping and thrashing.

Tryton raised his head again and met her eyes. There was something so powerful in the way he looked at her, something primordial and basic and masterful. He was a god when he looked at her like this, controlling her every move, her every emotion, her every feeling. There was nothing she could do against his will, she was his in every sense of his word. Looking at her this way, moving in her, taking her, he *owned* her.

"That's it," he urged, putting his forehead on hers. "Come on." His teeth were gritted.

Niki felt his pulse through the length of his cock. He swelled and surged inside of her. He filled up every empty space she'd ever had, until she was overflowing with him and there was barely any room for her anymore. There was only him…

She shattered and came completely undone in his arms.

He guided it, took it and gave it back to her. With the last desperate gasp and shudder of her release, he jerked free from her. A roar of male triumph echoed in her mind and in her heart. His head at her breast, his voice still echoing about the room, he spent himself on the sheets with violent abandon.

Minutes passed. Silence reigned. They rested, pressed tight together, his weight covering her like a protective blanket. His arms held her with such gentle strength that her heart flip-flopped crazily in her breast.

Tryton was like no man she'd ever met. He was strange, but he was…magical. He was more perfect a lover than she could have ever imagined in a lifetime of fantasies. He was powerful and arrogant and incredible.

And she'd only known him one night…what was to come next?

He stirred against her. His hands stroked over her, coaxing and soothing now more than ever. "Jada is here," he murmured into her skin.

She started, reality washing over her like a cold rain. But he would not let her withdraw. He held firm, still petting her, still calming her in the aftermath of their passion.

Niki was nearly panicked. She needed to get dressed. She needed to see her baby and make sure she was okay. It had been three months since she'd seen her daughter, three long and lonely months in which she'd missed Jada terribly.

But the separation had been necessary. Niki feared for her daughter's life every day she spent with her. Damn, but she wanted to die. If only she could control her strange powers, if only she could have her daughter back forever, safe and sound as it should be. But she couldn't. And the risk of hurting the only person in the world whom she cared about was far too great to chance.

"Let me up," her voice trembled.

"Be calm."

Strangely she was, almost immediately, going still again beneath him.

"I'll get you some clothes. You can wear some of mine, though they'll be absurdly roomy. It will have to do until I can talk to one of our seamstresses."

"I have clothes at home," she frowned. Home seemed so far away now.

"Then we'll have those brought for you, but not just yet. There is much to be done." He sighed, rising from her as if with some regret. "Come. We'll return to this later."

Her insides clenched and, god help her, she felt the wet pool of arousal between her legs surge once again.

His eyes met hers for one last, lingering gaze and she knew—damn him—that he was fully aware of her response. He smiled knowingly, arrogantly, and moved to get her clothes from his wardrobe.

She cursed and rose to join him.

Chapter Eight

"If you send me back to school, I'm going to tell everyone about this place," Jada snapped.

Tryton was taken aback. "What do you mean by 'this place'? This is my house," he lied.

The girl was too smart to fall for that, and that as much as anything else about her—she *was* incredible for a human child—shocked the hell out of him.

"Bullshit—"

"*Jada*," Niki reprimanded sharply.

Jada rolled her eyes. "Sorry," she huffed out, though she didn't sound sorry at all. "But I know you're lying, Mr. Elder. This isn't just a house, this is some kind of underground cult or something. I know it."

He nearly laughed. "No, it isn't like that at all."

"What is it like then?" she pressed.

Jada was so much like her mother; if he'd had a heart he would have already lost it to her. He shrugged, searching for the right words. "This is more like a sanctuary. It *is* my home, you know."

"It's not a house," she persisted.

"Not a conventional one, no." Really it was the size of a large human city, all of it, but he wouldn't tell her that either. "But I live here."

"How did I get here?" Jada pressed on. "Emily wouldn't tell me anything except to ask you."

"Grimm brought you."

"No shit, Sherlock—"

"Jada," Niki barked.

"I know he brought me here, but *how* did he bring me here? Is it magic?"

"Do you believe in magic?" Tryton asked her, curious to know her answer.

Jada shrugged, her shining brown hair—unlike her mother's more textured curls—shimmered with her every movement. "Maybe." She looked at Niki pointedly, and Tryton knew the girl was fully aware—despite all of Niki's caution—of her parent's secret.

"I think you do," he offered.

"Tryton, I don't think this is a good idea," Niki started to warn him.

He ignored her and continued, his gaze centered solely on Jada's. "I think you believe in all sorts of fantastical things."

Jada cocked her head and frowned, eyes going hot with some unnamed anger. "Mister, your tone is far too deprecating and I don't care for it. I'm not a baby you have to talk down to."

Tryton felt his eyes widen. She seemed as adept at surprising him as her mother.

Jada looked back and forth between him and Niki. "I might believe in magic. Not the whole rabbit-out-of-a-hat, or the-world-is-our-mother-let's-praise-her, kind of magic. But…there's other stuff I've seen."

"You know about your mother," he said flatly. "I can see it in your eyes."

The girl smiled a tiny, enigmatic smile and for a moment both Tryton and Niki saw a shadow of the woman Jada would grow to become. But then it was gone and in its place was an impatient, stubborn, intelligent youth. "I'm not an idiot—of course I know."

"Baby, you don't understand," Niki cajoled, trying her best to rescue the situation. "Not all of it."

"I know you send me away because you're afraid of hurting me." Jada's eyes dared Niki to deny it.

Niki could not. It was, after all, the truth.

"I know you can help people. Not like it was before—when I was little and you were just a nurse—it's different now. You help them, I mean *really* help. Cuts and scrapes and colds go away when you touch people. You can 'think' someone well, and somehow they get well."

Niki nodded, looking down, away, anywhere but into her daughter's too wise eyes. She'd never known how transparent she'd been to her daughter before now. She'd always been too afraid to broach the subject, too protective and worried how it might affect Jada emotionally and mentally.

Jada reached out and surprised them all by touching her mother's hair comfortingly. "You've hurt people, too. I know. But it's not your fault," she continued in a rush, "I know it's not. I know things sometimes, I really do. You didn't mean to hurt them, you were really trying to help but you didn't understand how to do it right."

"I didn't want you to know," Niki admitted hoarsely.

"I know that too. But something's happened now, and the cat's out of the bag for everybody." Jada pulled back, settling into her chair with a sigh that sounded far too old from one so young. "Isn't it?"

"Yes," Tryton answered for her.

Jada's eyes flashed at him. "What do you have to do with it?"

"I'm trying to keep your mother safe."

"From who?"

"From everything," he answered truthfully.

Jada thought for a moment. "Are you saving her from me?" she asked with some noticeable difficulty. "Do you want her to stop seeing me? Or doesn't she want me anymore?"

Tryton saw the fear in her eyes and felt a searing pain in his soul that he had caused it, however unintentionally. "No, never," he swore. "Your mother loves you more than life. While I keep her safe, I would keep you safe as well, but never would I come between the two of you."

Jada sighed. "You're her boyfriend?"

He smiled. "Yes. A little."

Jada smirked. "A little? You either are or you aren't."

"He is," Niki said, surprising him.

"You love him?" Jada baldly asked Niki.

Niki looked at him wildly, panicked, as if she didn't know exactly how to answer.

"Yes, she loves me," he said arrogantly, sure that eventually those words wouldn't feel like lies on his tongue. "And I'm going to take care of you both."

"I don't need taking care of," Jada snapped.

"Maybe not, but Niki does. She needs me, to teach her to control her power, to keep her safe."

Jada nodded sagely, agreeing.

Niki choked and sputtered, clearly trying to hold her tongue in check in front of her child.

"Okay then," Jada said finally, as if she'd reached a decision that had been plaguing her. "If you take care of her, I'll go back to school. But I want to see her more often," she warned, far too much the adult for his comfort, given the situation. "I don't want to go months at time without seeing her anymore."

"Baby, I love you, I wanted to see you—you have to know that—but I wanted to keep you safe more than anything." Niki had tears in her eyes and voice.

Jada softened and again there was the hint of the woman in her. "I know Mom. I'm sorry I was such a pain. I'm not really mad about it, 'kay?"

Niki nodded, beyond words.

"Can Grimm take me back?" Jada was an excited young girl again.

Tryton felt overwhelmed and completely out of his element. He couldn't wait to officially claim the imp as his child before the Council. But there were other matters to attend to first.

"I don't think you should go back to the same school." He realized it would be foolish to take the risk that the Daemons might track her there. Niki's eyes widened with panic and he quickly moved to ease her. "There are better, more prestigious schools, after all," he hedged.

"What are you, rich or something?" Jada snorted.

"Yes I am." He had never been proud of it, but there it was. He was partially responsible for the structure of the human economy after all, and had unlimited funds in all currencies at his disposal. For the first time, money meant something to him beyond the means to an end. It meant security for his family. "How does a trip to Europe sound?"

Jada's eyes bulged. "Wicked."

"I'll have Emily make the necessary arrangements at the best school available. You can leave tonight and we'll have your belongings shipped from the Seattle school posthaste." He paused. "As well as a healthy allowance to get you anything you should need."

"Cool." Jada smiled and looked over at Niki mischievously. "Way to pick a winner, Mom."

Tryton had never felt so powerful.

* * * * *

"You didn't have to do that," Niki said as they walked back to Tryton's rooms.

"I know," he said simply.

"Why did you?" She frowned.

Tryton remained silent, walking steadily so that his footfalls echoed in the incredible stone corridor.

"Damn it, just tell me, why did you do it?" Niki demanded again, halting stubbornly in her tracks until he did the same.

Tryton turned and eyed her for a long, intense moment before he answered simply, "Because she is a part of you, and as such, she is mine. I always take care of what is mine."

"No." Niki shook her head jerkily. "That was just sex talk between you and me, a way for you to coax your way into my punani. It was fun then, but not now, not out of bed. I don't belong to you, and my daughter certainly doesn't either."

"Punani," he breathed the word, shocking her into silence by swiftly backing her up against a wall, towering over her effortlessly. "Punani. I like that word very much. Punani." It sounded so exotic on his tongue, even to her ears. "What does it mean? As if I couldn't guess... Though human slang is ever-changing, its roots will always be the same no matter what language is used." He took her hands and raised them above her head, clasping her fingers in his.

"I'm not having this discussion." Was that her voice all breathy and rushed? "We were talking about why you just spent a fortune sending my daughter to a school in— oh god, I can hardly believe it!—*Switzerland* of all places."

Tryton ignored her. "Punani...punani. It's like syrup on my tongue." He bent to her neck and inhaled deeply, breathing her in.

Her stomach clenched at the double entendre. "Stop it." His sensuality was overwhelming her, just as it had every second since their meeting. "You're making me crazy."

"Yes, so you've said before. But," he put a finger to her lips when she made a move to speak, "I took care of our Jada, did I not? I have provided for her future and her safety. There is nothing more that need concern you about her, but your love for her."

"I do love her," she managed defensively.

His eyes glowed in the dim light of the corridor. "I know you do. You've worked hard enough to keep that love alive, despite the dangers you encountered along the way. And I applaud you. But your struggle is over now. Now you may love Jada as a mother should, with no more caution. I have things well in hand on all other fronts. You will have no more worries about your powers, about your problems, about any of it. I won't allow it."

Niki nearly choked on her shock. "You won't allow it? You won't *allow it*? How can you have control over something like that, you, you....*ooooooh!*"

"I sense you are a little agitated by all this," he teased. "But you will grow accustomed to it."

"I want to go home," she bit out irrationally.

"No you do not. You want me to pull those too long, too baggy pants of mine down around your ankles and take you here against the wall."

She gasped and sputtered. "You overbearing, arrogant, pigheaded son of a—"

He pressed his mouth against hers to silence her.

Her outrage gave way to burning, white-hot anger. Mixed with the arousal she felt with each press and nibble of his lips, it was a dangerous combination. She felt her power flash out, pulsing between them despite her desperate grasp for control of it.

Tryton groaned and shuddered against her. "Woman, you don't know what that does to me," he growled at her mouth.

But she did know and it confused and frightened and—yes, absolutely—aroused her.

"How can you react this way? I have killed three people with this..." she searched for a word and found none she liked, "this magic of mine."

"I am not a human." He met her gaze steadily as he said it, daring her not to believe him.

She already knew he was more than human. How could she not, with all the things she'd recently seen?

He squeezed her hands tight in his. "You need never fear this. Us. None of it. Let it come, let it be. I will take care of you, my goddess. I will take this power of yours and help you to control it, wield it, shape it into something we can both enjoy."

"Stop calling me that."

"Goddess? Why? It makes you wet every time I say it." He flashed his teeth in something resembling a grin, but it was just too dangerous an expression to ever be called such. "And I love it when you are wet."

She trembled against him and felt the surge of his erection press heavily into her belly.

"Elder?" A voice called out from farther down the corridor.

Tryton rested his forehead against hers for a moment before stepping back and looking toward their visitor. "Yes, Cady?"

A short, curvaceous woman approached and Niki felt her teeth gnash against her lips. Was every woman here beautiful? Admittedly she'd only met Emily — and that had only been a greeting and a handshake — but now there was this woman. Niki had never seen such beauties before. They just seemed to flock about Tryton — two beautiful women were two too many.

And she was, inexplicably, jealous as hell. *Damn* it.

"We need to meet. There've been some…" She cleared her throat, her golden eyes flashing from Tryton to Niki and back. "There have been some questions raised. I don't think you'll be able to avoid answering them this time."

Tryton remained poised, even though Niki heard the censure in Cady's voice. Was it there because she disapproved of his dalliance with her, or because of something else?

"Yes. Call a meeting. I'll be waiting."

Cady nodded, turned, and continued down the corridor with purposeful steps.

"What's going on?" Niki asked.

"You are taking this transition well." Tryton took one her hands in his again and led them back towards his apartment. "But I've much yet to tell you. I don't know how you'll take it all in...but just remember that no matter what you hear this day, what is between us is more truth than any of it. All right?"

Niki frowned. "We had sex after only one night of knowing each other. I think I'm pretty open-minded at this point."

"You'll have that belief tested in the coming hours, I promise you."

"What's going to happen to me? After this, I mean? Will I go back to my life? All those things you said to Jada—"

"Were true," he interjected. "Your life is with me now. I'll take care of everything, always, do not concern yourself with that."

"How can you say that? You don't even know me."

Tryton stopped before her again, facing her with that intensity in his gaze that scared and excited her so. "I know enough. And so do you. Do not deny it, you feel it," he placed a hand over the beating of her heart, "in here. You may not understand it or rationalize it, but it's there. If you went back to your life now, the Daemons would surely take you. The thought of you placing yourself in such unnecessary danger whilst I am here and ready to protect you maddens me. Here, I can keep you safe. Here, I can keep you in my arms and in my bed, where you belong. You are not going back to your old life, all of that is over. You and Jada are mine now, my family, and under my protection."

Niki reeled. "I don't like this," she gasped, shaking.

"You will get used to it."

"Fuck you," she spat, stunned nervousness giving way to hot anger. He was by far the most arrogant man she'd ever known! But he wasn't a man...not really. He was something else entirely. "Fuck you," she said again, weakly this time.

"We will get to that if, gods willing, we have enough time before the others arrive." He clutched her hand in his, and lengthened his strides so that she had to trot to keep up with him or else be dragged along behind him as they covered the last of the distance to his private apartment.

Oh shit, what had she gotten herself into? She worried that she wasn't even beginning to understand the full extent of the dangers associated with this man and these people, these Shikars.

Heaven help her, for she was powerless, caught up in the clutches of the beast. And Tryton wasn't about to let her go now that he had her. The door opened and he pushed her unceremoniously inside, into his lair. He followed, slammed and locked the door shut behind them and then turned to tower over her.

She was unavoidably trapped, and there was nothing she wanted to do to change that.

Chapter Nine

One second he was feet away from her, staring at her like a predator eyeing his next meal. The next, he'd caught her up in his arms, forcing her mouth open to accept the sweeping caress of his tongue.

His kisses were like drugs and she was so addicted that she knew she'd need therapy to kick the habit.

He took her hand and placed it on his cock, which he'd already nimbly freed from his trousers. "Touch me," he rasped.

Niki had to, he felt too good to protest. He was thick, so hot and heavy in her hand. She had to stroke him, she had to clasp him in her hand, and oh, god she felt his response to her touch like a flood of lava in her veins. He groaned, she pumped, he gasped, she squeezed—she'd never felt so omnipotent, so incredibly *female*.

"Quickly," he breathed, "the others will be here too soon to make it last. Unless," he swallowed hard when she stroked him from base to tip and back, "you want them to watch."

It shocked her to the core—he sounded completely serious about that. He must have exhibitionist tendencies—but she did not, or at least none that she knew of. Voyeurism she could do, but not the other. Not yet anyway, she almost smiled, but his tongue was in her mouth again and she couldn't get past the wild, delicious taste of him.

His hands were busy pushing her pants down and off. His mouth was eating hers, stealing her breath. She couldn't keep her hands off him, and when he pushed her away she growled her impatience, surprising them both with the fervency of her excitement. Tryton grinned, baring his teeth wolfishly, then pushed her back against the door.

She screamed her shock as he lifted her high, placed her legs over his shoulders, and buried his face in her pussy.

His tongue speared her, laved her, lapped her up. Niki had a wild moment when she was thankful to have recently waxed as Tryton nuzzled his nose, mouth and chin deep into her wet sex. The sheer strength in him was astounding. He held her immobile, high over his head with the door at her back, steady and open for his wicked kiss.

The silky, cool feel of his hair tickled her from thigh to toes.

"Mmmmmm," he vibrated against her clit, making her wince and cry out from the sheer torture of it. "I love the taste of your punani. I knew it would taste just like a ripe, juicy piece of fruit." His tongue licked a long line from her hole to her clit.

She whimpered.

"They're coming," he rasped against her, kissing her quivering, wet flesh. "But you have to come first."

Somehow, he covered her entire pussy with his mouth, sucking on all of it at once, while one of his fingers probed gently at her anus. The tickling, massaging feel of him down below on her ass, the pull and draw and sucking of his mouth on her cunt, made her shout and bear down on an explosive orgasm that took her completely by surprise.

Her juices wet his face, and he lapped her up like a bowl of cream. A knock on the door behind them had her gasping, even as her orgasmic shudders still racked her.

In a whirl that had her head spinning—not just from her incredible dance into the stars—Tryton lowered her and redressed her in record time. He delicately adjusted himself back into the housing of his own pants, laced them both up securely, kissed her hard on the lips, wiped her juices off his face, and opened the door to greet the first of their visitors.

Niki just knew she was going to pass out—little black spots were actually dancing before her eyes. Tryton was too incredible for her own good health.

"Are we interrupting?" A tall, auburn-haired man entered the room, his hair thick and long, his bearing almost regally graceful.

Niki could see by the look on his face that he knew darned well the answer to that question, and he also knew exactly *what* he'd been interrupting. She thanked her lucky stars that her skin was so dark, if it hadn't been her blush would have been a red flag for all to witness.

"Niki this is Edge, and you already know Emily."

Niki nodded, getting over her embarrassment enough to notice the familiar woman at his side. "Hello again, Emily."

"Hello yourself," Emily grinned.

Niki's blush intensified. *Damn* it. "I thought you were taking Jada to school?"

"It's been done. It's amazing how quickly things move when a lot of money is involved," Emily chuckled. "I left her with Desondra to get settled in."

"Who's Desondra?"

"My aunt." A lithe man with short, white-blond hair entered the room, with an incredibly cute, violet-haired woman at his side. "Don't worry, Niki, Desondra will take very good care of your daughter," he told her easily.

"She's going to stay the first week with Jada, just to make sure she's comfortable with her new surroundings," Emily elaborated.

Tryton sighed heavily.

Cady marched into the room, her dark, fat braid of hair swinging about her hips. "I think Desondra's more worried about Zim discovering her secret than anything else."

"What secret?" Edge frowned.

Cady's eyes flared a second before she regained control of her expression. "Secret? What secret?" she recovered quickly.

But not quickly enough. "What are you hiding from me, woman?" An even taller man stepped through the door now, his ebony black hair hanging like a waterfall of silk to his bottom. "In fact, what is going on here lately? All the secrets, all the intrigue, it is giving me a pain of the head."

"You don't get headaches honey, you're not a human," Cady gibed.

Niki reeled. So many volatile personalities here, in one room, were making her head spin. Or maybe it was the lingering effects of Tryton's seduction—she could still feel the press of his tongue between her legs...*oh hell*. Her legs nearly buckled.

"Niki, this is Cinder, Steffy, Obsidian, and Cady. These, along with Grimm — whom you've also met — are the members of my personal team of warriors. They are the best of the best outside of the Council, the most powerful fighters ever produced amongst our people."

Warriors? *Fighters*? What the heck was this, some kind of commando camp? "Hello," Niki managed weakly. Just what had she gotten herself into here?

"Sit, everyone, please." Tryton motioned towards the comfortable chairs and couches that were gathered about the enormous fireplace set into the earthen, rock wall. "We have much to discuss."

"You are damn right we do." Steffy marched up to him with pursed lips. "Grimm says you can explain this. I'd like that explanation now." She shoved a handful of material at him.

Niki strained to look at the bundle and was not a little confused when she caught a glimpse of some sort of badge nestled within the scraps of muddied cloth.

Tryton's hand closed about it, clenching into a fist that threatened to crush it, but he didn't bother looking at it.

"Please have a seat everyone. We'll start as soon as Grimm arrives."

"I want to start now," Cady flared.

"Be silent," Obsidian told her impatiently, only just softening the command with a warm and loving look. "We've waited this long. Now we will all await The Traveler and begin the meeting properly."

"Let's be honest, Grimm already knows more than we do — a lot more — so why should we wait?" Emily pointed out. Edge seemed to be pushing her towards the couch, trying his best to quell her without saying a word.

Luckily, Grimm chose that moment—right before the volatile tempers of the women erupted completely—to appear in their midst.

Tryton took a deep breath. "Can we all agree to hold council together now, honorably and respectfully, as we have in the past?" He waited for their agreement before he continued. He even included Niki, as if she were already an accepted member of their group.

"I know you have many questions that need answers. You already suspect some of those answers, else you would not be so demanding and suspicious, but I thank you for coming to me before you speculate amongst yourselves."

"Just answer me this," Obsidian said quietly. "Have you had these answers all this time? Were you knowingly withholding information from us?"

Tryton was quiet for a long time. He led Niki over to a divan and sat with her there, his hand taking hers and holding it as if for support. Niki knew better than to be fooled—Tryton needed the support of no one. He was a law unto himself—that was more than clear. But it was nice to hold his hand all the same. She entwined her fingers with his, and was pleased when he gave her a reassuring squeeze.

After a long searching look at Obsidian, he answered. "I have always let you know what you must. True, there are some secrets I have always known and kept, but there are some that have only just been made clear to me." He gave Niki a glance out of the corner of his eye. "As is true in times of war with any people, I have kept my own council, but never have I sent you out into battle with less intelligence than what you needed to survive and triumph."

"You son of a bitch," Emily muttered.

"We have all known to some extent, Elder, that you possess knowledge which we do not," Cinder said formally. "But I cannot help but feel that you know far, far more than we suspected."

"Oh, he's always known more," Steffy told them all. "I've seen it in his eyes and in his heart. But he's never meant us any harm. For two thousand years he's led the Shikars into battle against the Horde. He's the most powerful man on the Council. He has our best interests at heart, but do not doubt for a second that he also has his own private agenda."

Niki reeled. Two thousand years? How was such a thing possible? Tryton's hand tightened around hers, nearly bruising her, as if he sensed her surprise and warned her not to withdraw.

"I would never see any of you harmed. I have brought you warriors together from childhood, to make of you my personal aides-de-camp. Cady, Steffy and Emily were perfect for our team from the first, and I admit to a little matchmaking on my part. I knew that together, all of you would help to change the very foundations upon which the Shikar Alliance stood, and you have. You *will*, I have every faith of that."

"You planned all of this from the first moment? Cady and Steffy and me, I mean?" Emily gritted her teeth, eyes blazing.

"Not all of it," Tryton admitted. "You, for instance, were a complete surprise for reasons you already know. I would have accepted you into our ranks without your being a Shikar, I've told you that. It was…unexpected that you become one of us."

Niki sighed heavily. "I'm completely lost here."

"All in due time," Tryton murmured, pressing a kiss to her forehead.

"Are you going to tell her before you change her, or are you just going to do it without worrying about how she might feel about it?"

"Cady, that's enough," Obsidian admonished.

"What are you talking about?" Niki frowned.

"Hasn't he told you yet?" Cady sneered.

Obsidian caught at his wife's hand. "Stop it."

"Why? He's always played around with our lives, why can't we return the favor?"

With every word from the woman, Tryton flinched. No one would have seen it, no matter how hard they looked, but Niki could feel it in him and it made her wild with protective anger.

"From the way it looks to me, you're all acting like spoiled children. If, as you say, Tryton is such an incredible leader, you should at least wait to hear what he has to say before you rail at him. In fact, you should all be grateful that he's willing to explain anything to you at all. It's his right as a leader to keep information from his subordinates. Especially if they're going to act as irrationally as you all are now, whenever he offers a little candid discussion."

There was a long stretch of stunned silence in the wake of her outburst.

"She's right," Edge murmured. "We are all overzealous. We must be patient."

"It always takes a fresh eye to see and point out the full extent of our foolishness," Cinder added. "Thank you for that, Niki."

"I'm sorry, Tryton," Cady subsided. "I'm just a little stressed out. The thought of so many secrets... I admit, I've been waiting for the other shoe to drop for years now. I shouldn't be so eager to disrupt everything we've worked for."

Apologies echoed around the room.

"Thank you, Niki," Grimm's voice surprised her. He'd been silent through all of it thus far.

"I will answer all of your questions before this is through. But first, Niki must tell you her story—" Tryton held her hand firmly when she would have pulled away in protest, "and we must make our move to save someone very dear to us. Someone who needs our immediate help, far more than you need answers."

"What is it?" Emily frowned, but there was a deep shadow dwelling in her eyes, as if she had some suspicions of what Niki might have to say.

"Begin at the beginning, my goddess," Tryton said softly for her ears alone.

"I don't want to," she said.

"Sharing will help you heal. But above all, your story will help my people save the world."

Everyone leaned forward and, with a huge breath of air to shore up her courage, Niki told them all she could.

Chapter Ten
Outside of Boston
Almost five years earlier…

"How long 'til we get there?" Niki called from the back of the speeding ambulance as she prepared the gurney for another patient. "This storm is getting out of control."

"A few minutes," Mitch, the driver, hollered back at her as he raced through a stop sign on the winding backcountry road.

"What have we got?" she asked, as they approached the grisly scene ahead.

"Car wreck, looks from here like it flipped. Only one vehicle involved. Some passersby called it in, I think. There's an injury, but I don't know how bad."

The ambulance hadn't even fully stopped when Niki jumped out of the back, medical bag in hand. Her eyes took in the scene with practiced exactitude. No detail escaped her, despite the cold, hard bite of the snowstorm.

A trail of debris was strewn from one side of the road to the other. The wreckage lead like a trail of bread crumbs to a mass of metal and glass that might once have been an economy-sized car, resting with deathly silence in a steep ravine off the shoulder of the road.

Niki wasted no time, uncaring of the cold powder soaking through her jeans. Inches of snow had already accumulated on the frozen winter ground, but not enough to cover the slight trail of blood she immediately noticed leading away from the car.

Mitch raced after her, yelling her name loudly to be heard over the screaming din of the wind. But Niki ignored him. She was focused solely on the droplets of blood that looked like bright red, juicy berries staining the white powder at her feet. She followed the sporadic traces of crimson, wondering in the back of her mind how there could be a blood trail but no footprints in the snow to accompany it. The meandering line of blood led into a dark copse of trees and Niki followed it, unafraid.

At first.

The tree line swallowed her up and the snow blew like an ice-cream cold tornado beyond it, whistling and howling, swallowing Mitch's calls. In the trees there was an odd sort of silence, an unexpected island of peace amidst the increasing violence of the storm. Niki strained her eyes, still following the blood, still intent on finding their injured patient wherever he or she may be.

Niki walked for a long time. Later, she would be astonished at just how far she'd traveled beyond the roadside, deep and distant into the woods. The cold bit at her, but was incidental in the face of her mission. She would not rest until she'd exhausted all possibility of finding a survivor. The blood trail grew heavier, a much darker and steadier line upon the powder-covered ground, and she knew she was at last drawing close to her quarry.

It never occurred to her just how someone losing so much blood had managed to pull themselves so far away from the accident scene. It didn't really matter. What mattered was that this person not die from blood loss or shock or exposure—or all three. What mattered was that Niki find them and fast.

She heard a strange noise up ahead.

Her heart pounded with some instinctive fear and she didn't know why.

Until she saw them…not fifteen feet away from her, moving like shadows amidst the gathering of trees and brush.

Large hulking brutes, they were. Disgusting and terrifying, with eyes like the brimstone and flames of hell, these monsters were growling and snarling. But not at her. Thank god, they hadn't seen her or she might have died then. Because they did not see her, because they were so intent on their task, Niki was afforded a healthy glimpse of them and the captive held within their midst.

They were dragging a woman, bruised and bloodied, to a gaping hole in the ground not too far ahead of them. Their lair, like pitch-black madness, mawed and seemed to beckon them. The monsters were tall, tall enough that the limp woman's legs dangled helplessly above the ground — and she was no petite bundle. The beasts themselves, though clumsy and ghastly, barely disturbed the bracken, snow and earth beneath their graceless steps. It was as though they were not part of the world around them in all ways, like spirits or ghouls.

That's why Niki had seen no tracks in the snow. They left none.

The woman, not long ago a girl in age, had long, tangled blonde hair. A wound on her head bled sluggishly, as did a cut on her cheek. But it was the jagged gash, the long crimson line from forearm to wrist, which bled most alarmingly. Fat, steady droplets fell, to sink into the snow, a pounding rivulet that only grew faster with each passing second, with each pumping heartbeat. It was this wound which had led Niki here.

If she didn't get the woman away from them, get her some help right away; she'd surely bleed to death.

But how could she save her patient from...monsters?

Suddenly the woman's eyes snapped open. Cornflower blue was all Niki could think. So blue, so clear, so deep. The color swallowed her world and burned her mind.

Run.

It wasn't Niki's voice, but the woman's, that shouted the word in her mind. An exotic scent, the perfume of wild jasmine and vanilla blossoms, ginger and rose, assailed her senses, making her dizzy.

Niki tried to scream, but no sound came forth from her cold-numbed lips.

She took a step forward, but something—some force or unnamed energy—held her back like a restraining hand upon her chest. The woman's eyes drifted closed, her face going slack.

Get away, run away, while you still can.

The words came with a jolt this time, an electrical pulse that shocked her muscles and her bones and made her hair stand on end. Niki felt and saw the ground rise up to meet her, and only managed to scream minutes later, when she woke up in Mitch's arms.

* * * * *

"No one believed me when I told them what I'd seen. No one would listen. There was a search party, just some good Samaritans who volunteered to look for her once the snow had died down. But of course no one found her.

Those monsters—the Daemons as you call them—dragged her down into that hole with them. And wherever they took her, she couldn't have lasted long after that. She was bleeding pretty bad.

"I found out a little about her later, but not as much as I would have liked. I wasn't a cop or anything and once I'd told my tale about monsters in the woods nobody was really willing to share much information with me. But I knew enough to realize that this woman changed me. Somehow she marked me, touched me psychically. I was never the same after that.

"I took leave from work. Just a few days. It was a week after I returned to work that I had my first accident. We were picking up an elderly—a heart attack patient, nothing out of the ordinary really. I was settling the woman onto the gurney when I felt this…I don't know, it's so hard to explain…"

"Try," Emily encouraged softly. Everyone in the room hung upon her words. The anticipation in the room could have been cut with a knife.

"I just felt this overwhelming warmth. All through me like a fever. With it came the smell of that strange perfume I'd scented around the woman and the monsters. My hands felt like they were on fire and when I looked at them they were bathed in light! The patient beneath my hands started choking. Her skin started to blister. Then she died. And it was all my fault.

"It happened again the next day, with another patient. A similar episode. And I knew then that I was different. Beyond different. I couldn't tell anyone about it. No one suspected a thing, thank god. Death was something we EMT's took in stride, it wasn't entirely abnormal that a patient die on the way to the hospital. But I knew. I knew it was me, and I got the hell out of there.

"I took my daughter and I moved back to Savannah, my hometown, to find some time to think. Unfortunately, I didn't get much time before the full extent of my danger became clear to me."

Niki fell silent, pensive, carefully choosing her next words. Would her revelation scare away these people, whom she so desperately wanted for her allies? Would it make her seem more the freak, more of a risk to them? She was afraid to go on.

Cinder leaned forward, perching expectantly on the edge of his seat. "So? What happened?"

Tryton squeezed her hand, urging her to continue. Though Tryton had accepted her story and assured her none of it was her fault, that none of it mattered, she felt sure the others would not feel the same as he. Tryton was an exceptional man. Niki could not expect such a reaction from his team. She took a deep breath and laid it all out as best she could, hoping she could accept their censure when it came. Niki felt sure it inevitably would.

"I got a job at a fast food restaurant—I was too scared to continue with my paramedic career. I walked to and from home for my shifts—traffic in Savannah can be hell sometimes, and I liked the exercise and the thick, humid air. Though my job wasn't in the best part of town, I never really gave much thought or caution to thugs. But I should have.

"As I was walking home one night—I'd had to work the closing shift, which I *hated* because it was so hard to find a babysitter for those hours—I ran into some trouble. I was mugged. It was a routine theft at first—if any theft can be routine. I gave the man my wallet. He should have moved on. But he got too close, he scared me a little too much.

"It was the fear that made me strike out. Hell, I didn't even know what I was doing, it just happened. One minute he was leaning in—I freaked out thinking he was going to rape me or kill me—and the next he was on the ground twitching. The heat, the perfume, it came on me like a flood and he was down. He was dead. And I had killed him.

"I enrolled Jada in a boarding school right after that. No way was I going to put my baby at risk. What if I lost my temper around her? What if she hurt herself on the playground and I got scared? How could I protect her from myself if my emotions got out of control? I didn't want her in danger—I couldn't put her in that kind of danger. She didn't understand. But I did it because I love her. I can't control it, even now, not like I should. And so I can't take any risks. I can't have any friends or family. I'm human and we all have emotions that we cannot control, only in my case people die when I give in to them."

"Jesus." Cady took a deep breath. "That's how you killed the Daemon. You let your power loose and down it went. No wonder they wanna kill you so badly—you're a bigger threat to them than we are."

"They don't want to kill her, Cady," Tryton murmured. "It's so much worse than that." He turned to look at Niki, his gaze taking in all of her before he spoke again. "Why don't you tell them the name of the woman you saw that night?"

"Raine Lansing. Her name was Raine Lansing and she's the reason the Daemons are after me. She's the reason I am what I am. And I, for one, wish I'd never tried to save her."

Chapter Eleven

Chaos erupted about the room.

Tryton tried to quiet them down, striving to keep some order amidst the shock and surprise of his team members.

Emily jumped from her seat and dived for Niki. Niki, shocked speechless at the woman's attack, jumped up and away, out of the Emily's reach. Tryton stepped between them, holding Emily back from her with a stern command. Edge rose behind them both, protesting his leader's hands upon his woman in no uncertain terms.

Steffy burst into tears, raving at Niki in thickly accented German. Cinder held her tight in his arms, even as she too struggled to rise and approach Niki with all the pain and rage in her heart.

Niki had expected a reaction, but none so explosive as this. She didn't understand why they were so incensed, so affected by what she'd told them, and her heart nearly broke with the pain of their displeasure.

Cady and Obsidian remained stoically silent, with pensive, thoughtful expressions on both their faces.

Grimm, for the first time, showed emotion, and none of them expected how volatile he could be.

"*Silence!*" He roared the command, his voice so loud and powerful that it echoed for many deafening seconds about the room.

Everyone was stunned into obeying him.

He flung his cowl back from his features, his hair more red than black in the light. His gaze, so black and so frightening, bored into Niki's. He came to her, putting his hands on her shoulders.

Niki was floored by everyone's actions, wondering what the hell had caused them to react with such violence. She felt Grimm's hands settle upon her, felt too how they shook with emotion, and her confusion and nervousness grew. Grimm didn't seem the type to feel any emotion, strong or otherwise.

"Are you sure her name was Raine Lansing?" He asked it with deceptive softness.

"Yes."

"How can this be?" he mused, as if to himself.

Niki shook her head. "I don't know. I don't understand—"

"Quiet all of you, and I will try to explain what I know," Tryton told them all, quelling the tide of their emotions.

"How is this possible?" Steffy managed through her sobs.

"I was as shocked as all of you when I heard Niki speak the name Raine. But I have had more time to think on it and I believe the answer, the why and the how, is simple." He looked at Niki. "Are you all right?"

Niki nodded, as curious as the rest to hear what he had to say.

"Come, sit by me again," he urged.

They all took their seats, all but Grimm, who paced before the fireplace in a rare display of agitation. He was like a shadow, black and brooding and at war with his reflection upon the wall, full of pent-up energy that had no place in such dark confines.

"We all know that before the time Cady joined us, the Daemons were a threat, but essentially they were not half as powerful as Shikars."

There were nods all around.

"It's true that sometimes Daemons strayed into the Territories, the surface world. But it was not often and it was mostly accidental. But there came a change around the time Cady turned fifteen. That was when the Daemons began swarming, moving en masse. Like a tide of evil seeking release from the boundaries of their poisoned lands, they began creating backdoors from their dimension to the world of humans. They crept in the dark through the lands of humans and preyed on those few mortals gifted — or cursed as the case may be — with psychic gifts.

"Daemons feed on psychic energy. It keeps them alive. It enables them to create, to give birth as it were, to more and more of their kind. Without it they would all surely die. Until that fateful day when Cady stepped forth and accepted the weight of her great destiny, the Daemon Horde relied on their Lord Daemon for such great stores of energy."

"But Daemon disappeared for centuries — we know that much for certain. And his power is now withdrawn from the Horde — we know that as well. He's either dead or whatever, *that* I don't know," Cady pointed out.

"Exactly. I think it was around this time — when you were but fifteen — that Lord Daemon's support was withdrawn. I think something happened, and the Daemons suddenly found themselves without an ample energy source." Tryton grimaced. "I didn't see it before, but now I understand why the Daemons wanted not to kill you four women, so much as they wanted to capture you. They needed your energy, they wanted to live."

"But I wasn't psychic," Emily reminded him.

Tryton nodded. "And that is the tie that brought it together for me."

Grimm stared intently at his leader. "What tie?"

Tryton smiled. "Raine is not dead, my friend. That's the tie, the link, between Steffy and Emily and Niki. Cady was the catalyst, the first target, because she was so strong. But we got to her first, thank all the Fates. After Cady, there was Raine, and unfortunately they managed to capture her.

"We know that Raine was a strong psychic. The Horde took her and now they feed from her, keeping her alive, because *alive* she can continue to provide them with the energy that they need. In life she was a master of astral projection — hence the Daemons inherited from her the ability to Travel.

"She was friends with our Steffy, and knew that Steffy had psychic abilities of her own, though they were not so strong that the Daemons might have hunted her down on their own. But Steffy knew her, held her memory in her mind — hence the Daemons sought her out. That's why they were there in Germany, so close to Steffy's club that night.

"Emily was her sister, and though Emily had no real powers and therefore no real worth to the Horde, no doubt Raine's thoughts focused on her sister. The Daemons used those thoughts, those memories, that love that Raine possessed for her sister, and moved to find Emily like dogs on the hunt. That's why, after weeks of inactivity, the

Daemons suddenly surfaced in New York City, so close to our Emily.

"And now Niki...Niki was the last person Raine saw before being taken. And Raine imparted something of herself to Niki, giving her a bit of power. We know this is possible because she did the same with Emily, to help Emily become a Shikar. This power and the memory of her in Raine's imprisoned mind, made Niki the next target. The Daemons sought her out—captured her—but Niki was too powerful, too lucky, for them to keep her for long. She escaped and she came to us.

"And she knows the way back. Back into the lair of the Horde, beneath the paws of the Great Sphinx. She can lead us there, down into hell, and it is there that we shall finally bring the Daemons down."

Emily shuddered. "Raine would never willingly help them."

"There's no telling what kind of torture she's enduring," Steffy choked out.

"All this time, we've been running in circles," Edge said. "It was never about Emily, or Steffy or Niki. It was never about us, never about an overpopulation of Daemons. It was, and always has been, about Raine."

"Through her, the Daemons are more powerful. More intelligent. They are able to recoup their numbers more efficiently. They are being fed all the energy they need to rise up and become a real threat to us, indeed the entire world," Obsidian pointed out.

"But that doesn't explain the badge or the uniform," Steffy frowned.

Tryton breathed deep. "Do any of you really know what a Daemon is?"

Silence.

"Haven't you thought of it?"

"They're monsters," Cinder offered. "Spawn of the devil himself, Lord Daemon."

"No," Tryton shook his head emphatically. "They are so much more than that. They are flesh golems, resurrections of the dead, humans or Shikars returned from the dead, reanimated—but poorly so. They are shells, pieces and parts of living flesh, put together by their creator." Tryton ran a hand through his hair erratically, gritting his teeth. "I can't explain—"

"Tell them everything, Elder." Grimm spoke into the roar of the flames, clenching his hands around the elaborate curves of the fireplace mantel. "Tell them all and be damned to these secrets."

"Hold your silence, Traveler," Tryton snapped. "You let your heart move your tongue, but hold to caution. I see no need to tell all."

"You're saying that Daemons are like zombies or something?" Cady clarified, ignoring the volatile mix of emotions that threatened to set fire to the room.

"Something like that," Tryton nodded. "Yes, very like that."

"And Niki can lead us into the heart of their lair?"

"Yes." Glad at least to be able to contribute to this part of the conversation, Niki answered her. "At least I assume that's what it was. It's not all that hard to find, once you know where to look."

"Then what the fuck are we waiting for? Let's go out and stop this war right now," Cady exploded.

Tryton looked at them, each one in turn. "I do not know what we will find down there."

"The truth." Grimm stalked over to Tryton, moving as silently as a sigh. "And the truth has never been anything you should fear, my friend. You have fought this fight for millennia…it's time to let it go."

Tryton nodded and held tight to Niki's hand. "We'll go at dusk. When the sun falls low over the horizon of Egypt—it's only midday now—we will finally put an end to this. Just us, our team, our family, as it should be. And may all the gods help us in the doing, for we're surely going to need it."

Niki shuddered and knew that, come good or come ill, her world would change forever with the coming of the Egyptian night.

It had already changed so much.

What more could happen, she didn't know.

Hell, she didn't *want* to know.

Chapter Twelve

When the last person had left, Tryton closed the door behind them and leaned heavily against it.

"You have many questions," he said, voice muffled, forehead resting against the ornate wood of the door.

"I don't know what the hell is going on anymore," she admitted. "But I'm willing to go a little farther on faith."

Tryton chuckled but it was a mirthless sound. "I've never met anyone like you before, human or Shikar. You don't seem surprised by anything. You don't seem to hold any disbelief in your heart."

"I've seen a lot," she admitted, "and done more. But if it hadn't been for that night in the blizzard I probably wouldn't be so understanding. Seeing monsters and being 'tetched' by Raine, has somewhat skewed my perceptions."

"Understandably," he chuckled again, sounding weary and drawn. "But I can sense you want to know something."

"I do have one question."

"Ask it." He seemed to steel himself in anticipation.

"If those women were once human, how did they become like you?"

He was silent for a long time. "It is not for you," he said at last, as if the words were difficult and painful for him.

"What do you mean?" she frowned. "I'm just curious. How did it happen?"

"I won't!" He slammed his fist with sudden violence against the door, and she jumped. "I won't do this."

"Do what?" she asked in surprised exasperation.

"This, this, all of this." He shoved away from the door, raking his fingers through his hair. His eyes, when they met hers, were haunted and filled with raw anguish. "I won't love you," he said, shocking her at last.

"I never asked you to," she responded defensively, even as her heart thumped and ached with a suspicious, yearning disappointment.

"Well I won't. I *can not*," he gritted, shaking his leonine head back and forth so that his hair was a halo of white-gold shimmering about him. "I won't."

"You've made that clear," Niki gritted out. "But you've ignored the most obvious truth here. And it's that you already *do* love me."

Tryton sank back against the door, his knees giving out under him, his eyes a burning sea of unshed tears.

"Whether you want to love me or not is irrelevant. Just as it's irrelevant what I want out of all this. I don't know you, Tryton. I don't know where any of this will take us over the next several hours—and if we survive that, then the next few days, weeks, months and so on. But I do know this—there's something in you that calls to me. There has been from the first. And it's the same for you with me. We're meant, you and I. There's nothing you can do about it."

"I don't want to love you," he whispered. "I have no heart, I have no love."

"You can keep telling yourself that all you want, but it won't change a damn thing. You'll just look foolish after a while. Accept it, you do love me. Don't you? Admit it."

He buried his face in his hands. "You don't know the danger of what you're asking. I cannot do it."

"What danger is there in love?" She moved to his side, running her hands down the length of his silken hair.

"You can ask me that, after you've spent these last years protecting your daughter from that very thing?"

"But to love my daughter could mean her death." She pursed her lips, eyes blazing at his reminder of it.

"And what do you think my loving you could lead to?" he shouted at her, jumping up to pace before her. "I killed my heart long ago, there's nothing of it left. There can be no more risks, not for me."

"What are you talking about?"

"You wanted to know how Cady and Emily and Steffy became Shikar? They died to their lives and were reborn to ours," he shuddered. "They were lucky. More lucky than they know."

"I don't understand where you're going with this." She slowly rose to her feet, meeting his gaze as best she could. There was such raw pain there, such suffering. She wanted to go to him, offer comfort, offer strength, but something held her at bay.

It was fear. Elemental, instinctual and strange, but there it was.

"You could die from my love. I won't put you in that danger. You, of all people, must understand this."

"You've lost someone before," she stated, hating the pang of jealousy in her heart. The knowledge that he had loved before, when he would deny her now, made her very soul weep with sorrow. "Haven't you?"

"I won't lose you." His eyes were pools of endless suffering.

"I won't let you," she promised, without knowing how she could offer such a promise. One never knew what the morrow would bring...or the next coming hours.

He swept her up in his arms, holding her tight, resting his face against hers. "I will always keep you, always be faithful to you. Jada will want for nothing, for she will be my daughter as well as yours. Neither of you will every want for anything else, ever. But do not ask me to love you. Please, I beg of you, do not ask that of me."

Her heart was breaking. What could she say to this? How could she respond? She didn't know her own heart, her own needs, but she knew that she wanted his love. And here he was, warning that he would never give it.

She'd seen him with Jada. Seen the light of adoration in his eyes when he'd looked at her—a father's love for his daughter, pure and shining and bright. She'd seen the acceptance in her daughter, seen the possibilities with Tryton that she'd never seen with Jada's birth father.

There'd been such pleasure, such joy in his arms and in his bed. He was a lover unlike any other. Powerful and strong, yet tender and gentle. Demanding and careful of her pleasure, *hers* above his.

He was the first person she'd known—since becoming what she was—who had understood her. He even understood her powers—when she did not fully understand them herself. There was no fear, no danger of her harming him when she lost control. Indeed, he seemed to crave it from her, the power that had always been such a curse to her in that regard. There would be no accident with him, no shadow of doubt that she might not be able to hold her power in check at those most crucial moments. With him she could lose her temper, lose her patience, lose her heart.

There had been so much between them from the start, mostly chemistry, mostly lust, but also something else. Something terrifying and exhilarating that had grown with each passing moment to overshadow even the lust and the wanting and the pleasures of the flesh. It was a pleasure of the soul and of the heart. But was he seeking to kill it now, when it had only just begun to burn so hot and grow so strong between them?

"I won't let you hold it back from me." She came to the decision the moment the words were said.

"You can't make me love you." He squeezed her tighter even as he rejected her.

She laughed, feeling stronger of a sudden, feeling better than she had in years. "I can and I will. I already have."

"I don't want to love you."

"I don't care." She squeezed him back, clutching his broad shoulders as the light of her love enveloped them both.

And there *was* light. Tons of it, stunning, bright gold. Emanating from her to him and back again. It was the light of her power and her strength, and for the first time she was glad of it. To see it, to know it, to feel it pulsing through her and him and between them like a river of warmth.

If she could heal all wounds physical...perhaps she could heal this one wound of his, this spiritual scar that he carried deep within. She poured her love into her power, let it feed the light, let it push with all her might into him and through him.

"I love you," she said. "I do. I would have never thought it possible. But you are mine. And I am yours. And no matter what happens, this will not change between us. You called me your goddess, and now I will adjure you as such. Heal, my Tryton, heal and love me. No matter what comes, no matter to any of it, we will have this and it will be enough. It will be more than enough. It will be everything and all things. Perfect and forever. I know it. Let your heart heal. Give it over to me. Love me."

She felt a hot, wet splash on her neck and knew that he wept. "I feared it. The moment I saw you, I feared it."

"Fear it no more," she said solemnly, meaning it, letting her power fade until it was no more than a lingering warmth. A memory.

"I can't hurt you. I can't risk it."

"We already have risked it, don't you see? Both of us. I love you already. For you to deny me now would hurt me far more than if you put a knife in my chest and left me to die. Let it go, the fear, the pain, all of it. I won't let you hold this back from me."

He pulled back to hold her face in his hands and meet her gaze dead on. His eyes, wet with tears and fierce with emotion, burned down into hers like twin flames, marking her to her very core. "Anymore, all I want is to be inside of you. Forgetting everything but you surrounding me, taking me deep, making me one with you."

This is so powerful, she thought, and realized she'd said it aloud. "I can't control it."

"I never could. I should have seen it." He swooped in for a kiss, parting her lips with his fiery hot tongue.

Thunder rumbled, a low, warning sound in the background.

A raindrop splashed onto her head and she gasped into his mouth. She jerked away in surprise, looking up above them, astonished to see the rain cloud hovering above their heads. A slow, drizzle of rain fell to wet their hair and skin.

"What the hell?" She breathed. The water tasted like him, crisp and fresh and magical. It fell on her face like a thousand moist kisses, like endless caresses, like tears.

"You make me lose control." He shuddered against her. Something like an electric shock sparked between them, her hair stood on end and her skin sizzled, and the rain cloud disappeared as quickly as it had appeared. "No one has managed to accomplish that in at least ten thousand years," he grinned.

She nearly choked. It took several tries to find her voice. "So I guess this is one of those May-December romance things."

"No. This is one of those forever romance things." He kissed her again and she forgot *everything*, his age, his power, everything but him.

The feel of him. The taste of his kiss. The scent of him — like a rain shower on a warm, spring day — it dominated her. His all made her feel weak and captivated, and she was. He was just too much at once, filling her up, flooding her through, until she was entirely his, unable to hold anything back. She didn't want to hold anything back.

She'd never felt so whole as she did there in his arms.

A blink and they were in his bed. He'd done that Traveling thing again and she'd been too lost in his kiss to even notice. God he was sexy when he used his magic—and for the first time she wanted to do the same.

Letting it gather, letting it build, was easy. It was so warm. Like his touch. Like his skin. It swelled within her, lighting them both up in a halo of gold that wasn't unlike his hair, that wasn't unlike his eyes.

"I'll make you forget her, forget the pain, forget that you've loved anyone but me," she swore.

He pressed his mouth to the pulse in her neck. "I've never loved anyone."

"But I thought—"

"I have seen love die. I feared it, that's why my caution with you. But I won't let that happen to you. I swear it. I could not bear it."

There had been such pain in his eyes before…perhaps he had not loved the same as he loved her—whether he said it aloud or not she *knew* he loved her—but he had definitely loved *someone* in the past. Niki knew it as surely as she knew her own heart.

Her power roared inside her head.

"Don't force it," he breathed into her Adam's apple, pressing tiny kisses there in between words. "You'll give yourself a headache."

Niki almost laughed. His conversation sounded so bland, when for years she'd been fighting with all her strength just to control her magic. How could he be so sure, so blasé, so wonderfully calm?

Because he was the same as she. He had such powers. And he knew how to command and master them. He was far, far more powerful than she could even imagine…but he only lost control when he was in her arms. It made her wet and heated, just knowing that she had this power over him.

A blink and they were nude. She didn't remember taking her clothes off, and she didn't know how he'd done it, but it didn't really matter. His kisses zeroed in on her breasts and that's all she could think about. All she could feel. Her nipples, long and hard, seemed to beg for his attention. He slurped one into his mouth and suckled it like a babe. The other he pulled and pinched delicately with his fingers until it ached deliciously.

Niki gasped and moaned and strained beneath him, wanting more.

"Feed your power, let it blossom," he said, licking her nipple to stabbing hardness before moving on to the other and taking it into his mouth greedily.

Her magic flared to life and burned her skin, just as his kisses did.

She moaned.

"That's it," he moved down, spreading her legs with the incredible breadth of his shoulders. He reached for one of her hands and brought it down between her legs. "Spread you punani, let me see your flower open and wet and *mine*."

She almost came, just hearing his words. Her fingers opened the plump lips of her labia, and she watched him watch her. His eyes never left her, searing into the heart of her. He seemed entranced. And god knew she was, just seeing him look at her like that.

"Such a beautiful pussy. So pink." He took the tip of one forefinger and traced it down the wet valley of flesh she held open for him. He pressed that tip into her, pushing in deep. "So tight. And hot. And wet," he leaned in and breathed over her clit.

"Oh god," she gasped.

"I was worshipped as a god more than once over the course of endless time," he murmured. "How fitting that you are my goddess, to share in that with me." He pressed a full, lips-teeth-and-tongue kiss to her quivering flesh. "Proud and powerful and brave. A warrior queen. With the finest pussy in all the world, and in all the history of the world."

He opened his mouth over her, sucking her, licking her. His finger pumped in and out of her in a slow thrusting that stretched and burned her but did not fill her nearly enough.

She wanted his cock.

He sucked nosily, the sound of it wet and earthy. If a sound could induce an orgasm, it would surely be the sound of his mouth eating at her pussy. He was incredible, shameless, voracious. She would have reflexively clamped her legs shut, but he forced them wide and open with his hands. Niki was stretched and splayed open for his pleasure and there was nothing she could do about it.

There was nothing she wanted to do about it. She lifted her cunt up into his face, urging him to bury deeper against her. He moaned against her and she nearly screamed. His teeth brushed over her clit and she did scream.

"I would make you mine," he said against her, almost a whisper that she could barely hear. "Make you like me."

"Then do it," she said, unafraid.

"You could die."

"What is love, if not the only real thing worth dying for?" she whispered, knowing it for the truth.

"I won't love you."

"Too late," she smiled.

"Feed your power, hold it tight," he commanded, a new urgency taking him, taking her, consuming them both.

He rose and flipped her over onto her stomach on the bed in front of him. He pulled her back against him, spreading her legs so wide it nearly hurt, hooking them back behind him as he sat there on his haunches. "You were born for this, for me," he said, sliding his cock hard into her from behind.

Niki screamed and clawed the flesh of his imprisoning arms until they pinkened and bled.

Tryton threw back his head and groaned, a long and animalistic sound that made her quiver with fear and excitement.

His cock stretched her so wide, filled her so deep, that she was sobbing with sheer, mad, painful pleasure. Uncontrollable and wild, it swelled and washed through her, as did the hot, hard length of him. There was no escape. No reprieve.

It seemed forever that he came into her. Forever until he rested at the heart of her. "I'm going to do it." He seemed amazed at himself. "I've made my choice."

She could only shudder and shake, impaled on his flesh and helpless with emotion.

"Make your power strong. It will carry you over," he warned, moving within her now. "Don't let it go. Don't let me go."

"Don't stop," she begged, mindless to all but his thrusts within her body, his strong hard body moving at her back.

The rub of the bedcovers burned her elbows. The hard skin of his legs burned the insides of her knees and thighs as he rode her, deep and steady at her back.

The slap of their skin was the only sound for a long while, but for the thunder of his power.

Suddenly, he leaned forward and shuddered over her. He held his arms clutched tight around her middle, moving her upon him with such easy strength it made her feel as helpless and weak as an infant.

"I *don't* love you," he mouthed at her neck. "I can't." His lips traced over her shoulders, neck and back, as hot as a trail of fire across her skin.

She felt the tickle and press of his fingers move down to seek out her clit. Her head fell back against him. He pressed hot, hard kisses to the side of her neck, that vulnerable expanse that seemed to have some secret connection all the way to her womb.

With each kiss, each rub of his fingers, each thrust of his sex into hers, she shuddered. She moaned. She sobbed and cried, and still he gave her more.

Suddenly he pushed her away, back onto the bed in front of him.

"I cannot do this, I *can* not!" he yelled the protest, voice anguished and beyond hopeless.

And Niki knew how to become a Shikar. It had been there for her to know all along, a mystery that was no mystery at all. She felt it in the mountain of restraint he had to exert over himself. Felt it when he tried to withdraw from her body after one, incredible last thrust.

No. She would not let him pull back now.

Niki shoved back at him with all her might, trapping him inside of her as she trembled on her hands and knees in front of him. She let the light of her power flood through them both, setting free all the last remnants of her control.

Tryton screamed like a jungle cat over her, his protest a wordless roar that deafened her.

Niki felt the wash of his come fill her, burn her, drown her. The next breath and she was there with him, caught up in a release so unlike any before it she began to fear that—yes, after all this, yes—she might die. She could die. She was dying.

And it was exquisite pleasure, this death, this end.

Cold.

Oh god…it was suddenly so cold she couldn't catch her breath. Pain and freezing cold, it filled her up. Her head ached with explosive violence. Even as the last vestiges of her orgasm slipped from her fingers, she was swallowed up in a horrible, shattering pain that ate the world.

But she felt his arms around her. Heard him calling her name. And the pain receded. Her magic was a light that flooded her vision. She was blind with it, blind with heat and illumination and lingering pleasure-pain. Her nostrils were filled with the scent of warm rain, her mouth choked on the taste of tears.

An electric shock raced from her brain to the rest of her body. Stars danced in the light before her eyes. She realized that all this time she'd had her eyelids closed.

She opened them.

"Welcome back," Grimm whispered down at her from his perch at her bedside and disappeared.

Still buried deep inside of her, still holding her tight with her back against his chest, Tryton wept.

Chapter Thirteen

"Tell me about yourself," Tryton breathed against her breast hours later as they lay together in his bed, warm and safe, cocooned in a billowing cloud of his plush coverlets.

It had taken this long to get her down from her high. After being turned from human to Shikar, caught nude and in flagrante delicto with Tryton by the stoic Grimm—who'd been summoned to save her—and realizing that nothing was ever going to be the same again...she felt a little excited tension was understandable.

"I still can't believe you called Grimm in here," she repeated for what must have been the hundredth time.

"Leave it," he clutched her tight. "He was the only one I knew who could try to save you."

"Did it never occur to you that I might have made it back on my own without his help?" she asked. "I've told you, I don't think I really died at all."

"You weren't breathing. I couldn't chance it. I had meant for him to be gone when you opened your eyes but—"

"I woke up sooner than you both thought I would. He didn't do anything to save me, he didn't have to, yes I know, we've been through it over and over again. I saved myself."

"I couldn't have chanced it. If I had known you would come back on your own, I wouldn't have called for him. But with all the other women—"

"None of the others were using their powers when they changed, were they?"

"I don't think so," Tryton admitted.

"I know so. I wasn't going to die, Tryton. I just know it."

"I was afraid," he admitted, pressing his lips against her nipple. He was resting full-length atop her, as if he was afraid she might bolt if he didn't hold her down. "Everything I'd ever feared had seemed to come to pass…and it was, all of it, my fault. Just as it had been in the past."

"Tell me about that, the past."

He stilled against her. "Not yet. I asked you first. Tell me about you."

She would have grinned at his evasion if she weren't so tired. "What do you want to know?"

"Who are your people, your family? Where did you come from? What's your favorite color, your favorite food—everything."

She did laugh then. "I don't think I can stay awake that long."

"Then just tell me a little bit," he pressed. His hands were petting down her sides, as if reassuring himself that she was still there, still safe, still in one piece.

"Well," she sighed, smiling, playing her fingers through his hair, marveling once again at how soft it was. "My mother was only fourteen when I was born, so my grandma raised me mostly. My mom, she had a lot of bad luck. My grandpa was the world to her and when he was killed in a robbery at the gas station where he worked, she just lost it. She was only twelve then. We were more like sisters when I was growing up than mother and daughter. She was into drugs and shit like that, making all the wrong choices, screwing up her life like so many other kids in her position.

"Being poor, the odds are stacked against you from the start. Especially where we grew up, in the south, in Savannah. My grandma, she tried to right in me all the things that had gone wrong with my mom. She taught me how to be strong, to be proud of who I am. To know what I want and how to work hard to get it. She was really strong."

"It sounds like she loved you very much."

"We were all close. My grandma had two sons besides my mom, younger than my mom, and she raised us all herself. She made us keep up our grades in school, encouraged us to further our education after graduation, even though she couldn't afford the bills that the grants and loans didn't cover. She worked hard right up to her death a few years ago."

"Did they know about what happened to you?"

"No. I never told them. I had moved away to Boston by then anyway, and I only saw them on holiday and reunions, so it wasn't too hard to keep it a secret. My uncles went on to join the military, to become officers, to get married and have kids of their own, and my mom died of an overdose shortly before my grandma."

"That is a tragic tale." Tryton soothed her with his hands and his voice.

"No." Niki shook her head, unable to let him think that. "I had a really good life. My mom had it rough, but she made the choices that got her where she ended up. Don't get me wrong, I loved her, but my grandma taught me that you have to work hard to make it, and my mom dropped the ball long before I arrived on the scene."

"You've always held true to the things your grandmother taught you. You've worked hard, despite the obstacles."

"I've had my moments of weakness. Too many. I've been tired, so damn tired I just wanted to lay down and die, but...if I had just given in and quit, I wouldn't be here. With you. With me and my beautiful baby girl given another chance to be together—even if I am a bit of a freak."

"We can live near Jada if you like, up on the surface."

"I thought you couldn't go out in the daylight," she frowned.

"I can. I'm from a different age than my Shikar brethren. Over the centuries, living underground, they have developed a genetic sensitivity to sunlight where I have not. And you have my DNA within you now, so though you are Shikar, you are also like me. You should rejoice in the sunlight, just as I do."

"Are the others jealous of you, do you think?" She knew she would be.

"They do not know. Well, most of them don't. Or if they know, they do not understand the why of it."

"How is that possible?" she scoffed, incredulous.

"Every few thousand years, I disappear for a while. Until the memory of me fades. Until, when I choose to return, there are none who remember me."

"Why the hell would you do that?" she exclaimed.

"Not all of us live so long as I have. Indeed, only Grimm is even close to my age."

"How can you know that?"

"I don't, not for certain." He frowned, and Niki could see the thoughts swirling behind his pensive gaze. "But none here, in this place, are as old as I. They know I'm old, but they've no idea just how old I am."

"Well? How old are you?" Her voice rose an octave with her surprise.

He paused for a moment, then laughed. "You know, I'm not certain anymore. I can remember the Egyptians. The Atlanteans. The Babylonians. Sumerians. Neanderthals are a vague memory—I might have been only a child still or they might have been a tale told to me by my mother. I don't know. My age can only be measured in my mind by the phases of human development and civilizations, years mean nothing to me anymore."

She didn't know what to say. What did one say to someone older even than Methuselah? Way older. "Are you—" she swallowed. "Are you serious?"

He nodded against her and her nipple hardened. The tip of his tongue darted out to taste it.

"Oh my god. Can you—are you immortal or what? Can you die?"

"I'm sure I could be killed. But…I don't know the rest. Do we, any of us, really know if or when we will die? Some of us grow tired and leave, to the shores and lands of the realms beyond, but if we do not grow tired, do we ever just stop? I don't know. I haven't."

"Humans die," she said emphatically. "They get old or they get sick or hurt and they die."

"Human souls never die," he reassured her. "Just as Shikars, they travel on to the lands beyond. But unlike us, humans do not take their bodies with them. They do not need them, I think. I think there are new forms waiting for them across the way. Stronger forms that do not weaken with age or illness."

"Will I die?" she had to ask. "Now that I'm like you?"

He lifted his head to meet her gaze. "I will not let you get hurt."

"But what if I get tired, as you said, what if I want to travel on?"

"Then I'll go with you," he smiled, unconcerned with that. Concerned only, it seemed, that she might be hurt and killed through unnatural means. "But I doubt you'll grow tired of this life any time soon with me around to keep you happy," he said arrogantly.

It seemed to her that Shikars viewed death as casually as they might view a sunset or a rain shower or a sneeze. It was, oddly enough, reassuring to her.

"I don't really feel too different," she admitted.

"You'll be faster, stronger, perhaps a little more intelligent. Your powers will be exponentially greater and you'll have a firmer control over them. Between Cady, Steffy and Emily, I've noticed that the effects are different from individual to individual after the change. No doubt you'll eventually show Caste traits just as they did."

"Caste traits—you mean like a race distinction or whatever? Huh. So what traits might I have?" she asked, curious.

"Well Cady is a multiple Caste, she is an Incinerator and a Hunter—she creates fire and can also track Daemons. Steffy is showing incredible skill with Foils. Emily, of course, is a Traveler. I think Raine had much to do with that. It was Raine, after all, who gave her sister the power she needed for the transformation from human to Shikar, for Emily was no psychic as a human."

"I get most of that—but what are Foils?"

He smiled at her mischievously and her heart tripped up to double speed. Tryton truly was the most handsome man she'd ever seen. And he was all hers.

He rolled from her and sat up in the bed, holding one arm out in front of him. Niki's eyes bulged when she saw his skin ripple alarmingly. Scant seconds later, long, glowing blue spines erupted from his forearm.

Niki screamed.

Tryton laughed and the blades disappeared. "Those are Foils."

"Holy shit! Didn't that hurt?" She turned his arm back and forth in her hands, inspecting his skin, looking carefully for wounds but finding none.

"No, not at all. When yours come in—they will whether you are a Foil Caste or not—then you will understand better."

"I don't want those things in me," she exclaimed.

He chuckled again and tugged on a lock of her hair teasingly. "Too bad, because they are part and parcel of being a Shikar. Eventually, you will get the hang of them. And of all the other things that come with your new life."

Niki's mind reeled. "So much has happened so quickly. I mean—" she looked around them, as if to find the words, "how long have I known you? I can't tell what time it is, day or night."

"Time does not matter so much to us. Sunlight and darkness are the yardsticks by which we measure time — and only then because we must. Urgency drives time, the Horde and their machinations give us that. Otherwise, we would be content down here, oblivious to the passages of the seasons on the world above. You and I have not known each other long at all — maybe, by your reckoning, a day, maybe a little longer."

"How can we be together like this in so short a time?" she marveled.

"Does it matter so much to you? Time?"

"No, I guess not," she admitted finally. "It's just a little unnerving when I really think about it."

"Do not think about it, then. You are probably still suffering from a little shock after all that has happened — there is no cause to dwell on it if you can avoid doing so."

She was silent for a while, reveling in the feel and scent of him sitting beside her in bed. For the first time in recent memory she felt completely safe. Completely whole and happy. It felt wonderful, almost too perfect to last. "Why are you so sad?"

"I'm not so sad now that I have you," he said, averting his gaze.

"You'll have to share yourself with me sooner or later."

He looked back at her. "I care for you," he said evasively. "Let that miracle be enough for now, my goddess."

"You love me," she insisted, knowing she was right when he shuddered at her words.

"Let it be," he pleaded.

She sighed and let the subject drop. It was enough that she knew the truth...for now. Eventually he would have to face facts but until then...

"If I am your goddess, why aren't you over here worshipping me?" she teased, rolling on her side so that her breasts were fully displayed for his hungry eyes to see.

"You're insatiable," he scoffed, pretending disinterest and doing a lousy job of it—his cock was at full attention already. "I think it's time you learned to worship a true god."

Niki laughed. "If you were worshipped as a god—I doubt *that*—which one were you supposed to be?"

He smiled enigmatically. "I was worshipped as many gods over time. Fuxi of the Chinese peoples, Poseidon— and his son Triton—of the ancient Greeks. Let's see...it has been so long...Erechtheus and Kekrops of Egyptian and Athenian lore. Ea of the Babylonians and Enki of the Sumerians. The list goes on, but I cannot remember many of them. Some of them were based on eyewitness accounts of humans who had seen me. Some of them were merely borrowed variations from other civilizations' texts. But trust me, woman," his eyes glowed rascally, "I *was* worshipped as god to many different peoples over the course of history."

"I'm sure you did nothing to dissuade them from worshipping you." She rolled her eyes. Inside, her mind was a whirl. Was he really serious? And if he was...*damn*, she was lying in bed next to Triton himself!

Tryton frowned then. "At first I did. I never wanted to be anything more than a man in those days. I walked the seas and the oceans, aided those in need upon the waves, but I did not do it with thoughts of grandeur in my mind. I'd always known humans to be weaker than us, and so I helped them. I had no idea it would come to disaster."

"What disaster?" She kept her voice neutral and quiet, careful not to startle him into closing back up after he'd opened this much to her.

But it was for naught. He shook his head, as if shaking off bad memories, and smiled at her. "We were never meant to interfere with human kind," he said at last. "I've let it go too far in recent times with Cady and the others. And now you." He shuddered, eyes going dark. "I've been selfish for my people and selfish for myself. I've been careless again. But things may change soon. I have you and that is enough."

"You do have me," she reiterated, hating the shadow that had crept between them in the past few moments.

"You might not want me after…" His gaze wandered, as if he were looking far away from her, from their bed and conversation. He cleared his throat once, twice, before he found the words. "After we go back to Egypt, you might change your mind about how you feel about us. About you and me."

She swallowed. "It has nothing to do with my mind, whether I love you or not. It has everything to do with my heart and my soul. There's nothing I could learn about you that could sway my heart from wanting you. Nothing."

"We'll see," he murmured.

He looked so sad, so beautiful and haunted; it nearly broke her heart to look at him.

"I want a shower," she said at last, to break the awkward silence, to put an end to the dark conversation.

He grinned. "Come with me." He took her hand and pulled her from the bed. "I'll have you so clean, it'll be only your thoughts that are dirty."

She felt her stomach flip-flop and laughed.

Chapter Fourteen

Niki looked about her, trying not to gape at the lavish bathroom he led her into. It was truly an exquisite work of art. Ornate, carved stone walls and marblesque floors in hues of turquoise and silver and white. In fact, the décor gave the illusion of moving, crashing ocean waves. It was dizzying to look about too quickly, for the illusion was almost perfect and overwhelmingly intense.

It was as big as a house, just this one room. The ceilings had to be at least twenty feet high. A sunken tub the size of an Olympic pool nestled in one corner. It was oval-shaped and quite deep.

"*Damn*, I'd hate to see your water bill for that thing," she said, incredulous at the enormity of it all. And she'd thought his bed was big.

Hell, everything about this man was enormous!

Tryton merely laughed. "Come here, let me bathe you."

"It'll take a week to fill that thing up," she pointed out.

"We won't be using that," he said, in all seriousness.

She eyed him suspiciously. "Not the thundercloud thing again? I'm not sure I want to risk getting struck by lightning."

He gave her a rakish wink. "Electrocution is definitely not the climactic ending I had in mind for us this rising."

She nearly melted on the spot.

"What kind of Caste are you, then? I mean, if you can create water does that make you a Water Caste?"

He ran his hand down her cheek, making her shiver. His gaze was so intense she could almost feel it, like a weight, as it roved over her naked form as she stood before him. "I am the only water power among our people. I am that rare oddity, a Shikar with no real Caste to claim."

"But you can Travel," she pointed out.

"Yes, but not with any great frequency as could a Traveler. I can also manipulate fire as do the Incinerators, but again it is a weak power in me. I can throw the Foils too, as Edge or Steffy might. No, I have no strong Caste traits such as those. My power comes from water. The wellspring of the Earth and the tears of the Heavens. Here, let me show you."

He bent to turn on one of the dozens of oddly fashioned faucets that arched over the rim of the tub like the long, graceful necks of giant swans. A long, crystal clear stream of water fell down, coaxed by gravity and by pressure.

But it never splashed down into the bathtub as it should have.

Tryton waved his hand over the stream and, like a viper to a snake charmer, it wove and undulated, reaching its way toward him. Tryton swirled his fingers in little circles and the stream twisted into spiraling tendrils, like little blooms and explosions of water all around him now.

Niki gaped and he turned to smile into her eyes. The water still flowed, streaming about his hands, arms and head. He walked to her, bringing his halo of liquid with him so that it moved to embrace her as well. Chaotic typhoons of it surrounded them, cooling the air surrounding their flesh, making their hair fly about with the rising force of the wind it stirred up with each passing stream.

Suddenly all the other faucets turned on—or maybe they didn't, maybe Tryton simply called the water forth from them, she wasn't sure—but within seconds, gallons upon gallons of water seemed to be flowing from the faucets towards them. Niki gasped and tried to pull away, but Tryton reached out and swept her tight against him. His gaze burned down into hers and she felt something low inside of her clench with yearning.

Not one drop of the water touched her or him. They were cocooned within the rushing, liquid tornado that now raged and swirled around them, standing together in the eye of the storm he had so effortlessly created.

He leaned down to brush his lips across hers. "Hold your breath, goddess," he smiled.

She took a huge gulp of air one scant second before the tornado collapsed inward and fell upon them with crashing violence.

Niki felt as if she'd been plunged head first into the depths of an ocean current. It swept her hair about her like a wild cloud. Tryton's blond locks caught and tangled with hers, a contrast of black and nearly white, yin and yang, male and female. She had to clench her arms about his neck to keep from being swept away. He cupped her breasts in his hands—an immovable bastion of strength in the water's fierce current—and kissed her hard and deep.

All of a sudden, the water around their heads was gone. The flow of it ebbed and changed. It opened up, like the petals of a flower, leaving her free and safe to catch her breath. Niki looked about them and was astonished to see that the roaring water raged only around them, like a cocoon encapsulating them, leaving the surrounding space untouched and dry. With another shock, she realized that her hair and skin, from the top of her head to her waist — where the water still swirled over her — was completely dry. Squeaky clean, dry and satiny, without a drop of dampness to prove she'd been completely submerged mere seconds before.

Tryton was the same, his long hair a platinum waterfall of silk down his chest and shoulders that gleamed fresh and soft and clean.

"Oh my god," she whispered, amazed.

He leaned down and sucked on her lower lip, taking her amazement and surprise into him, feeding on it with masculine pride. "Spread your legs," he commanded.

She must not have obeyed him fast enough, for the next thing she knew he was bending, reaching for her knee and raising it up to hook over and around his hip.

The typhoon of water swirled away. Tryton kissed her neck, scraping his teeth dangerously over her vulnerable skin. Over his shoulder she saw the water reshape itself and she shrieked.

"No way, *nowaynowaynoway*," she panted, heart racing, eyes wide.

"Yes way," Tryton chuckled, fingers moving to brush over her swollen clit.

The giant, crystalline phallus he'd created out of the water moved to position itself at the mouth of her pussy.

"This isn't possible," she gasped. But it was. The water-cock pushed its way into her, soft and warm, but still firm enough to let her feel every nuance of its shape and girth.

It began to thrust in and out of her. Tryton let go of her leg and bent to suck on her nipples. Niki shrieked again, the pleasure was almost too intense to bear at once.

Tryton's hands worked their way around her, sinking into the flesh of her bottom. He spread her cheeks wide and before she could find the breath to gasp a protest, a smaller, sleeker phallus made of water was inserting itself into her anus.

Liquid and warm, water filled every orifice but one. Niki had tears in her eyes and short screaming gasps on her lips as they thrust and stretched her over and over again, as Tryton's lips and hands worked on her breasts, belly, clit and ass.

She wanted him to feel some of this intense pleasure. But how?

Going to her knees before him, the water cocks still pleasuring her without missing a beat, she took his cock in her mouth and began sucking him.

Tryton shouted his surprise and pleasure, nearly collapsing before her.

His fists tangled in her hair, guiding her over him. His cock was so big, so thick, she could barely take the head of it, but he seemed to enjoy it all the same. Niki swallowed him to the back of her throat, careful of her teeth on him, even when he moved to thrust himself deeper into her mouth. Her spit wet him, wet her lips, and his cock shivered in her grasp.

Her hands pumped his shaft and cupped his testicles, plumping and rolling them until he was groaning and trembling. She looked up to see the long, clean line of his throat, his head tossed back, his chest and stomach muscles bulging with restrained ecstasy.

The water cocks shivered and disappeared, splashing inelegantly down about her legs as she knelt there on the floor. With a secret smile, that she could make him lose control where no one else could, she took his sac into her mouth, slurping and licking him greedily.

She lapped her tongue up and down his shaft, sucking on the tip as she passed it each time. Reaching around him, she played with his anus, gratified to hear him nearly scream as he thrust his dick deep into her mouth and spasmed.

One hard thrust made her see stars. And then she tasted the flood of him on her tongue as he came in a violent burst that washed clean down her throat. He was sweet and spicy and incredibly masculine. The delicious essence of him held a wealth of magic and mystery and she vowed to waste not one precious drop. She wanted all of him, filling her, flavoring her tongue, to remember forever and ever, come what may.

With a last spurt and a long, low moan, he fell upon her, spreading her legs. His phallus, still so hard and large, probed at her pussy. Niki gasped, unable to believe that he was still capable of such hardness after such a release. With a shudder, he thrust into her, and began riding her in that primal rhythm that drove her wild.

His eyes were vague, but they stared down into hers unflinchingly. With each pump and undulation of his hips, she gasped, shrieked. His body dwarfed hers, covering her, heating her, filling her up completely. The water beneath them shimmered and moved. Niki screamed as Tryton fashioned the liquid into dozens of little mouths that sucked and pulled at her skin.

From head to toe the mouths worked, while he thrust his body into hers with increasingly jarring movements. Niki felt her eyes roll back in her head. Tryton's forehead rested on hers and the liquid mouths pulled and sucked at her nipples, clit, and anus, even the backs of her knees were pleasured by the water he commanded.

His mouth met hers, his tongue delving deep. His kiss was like a lightning bolt, a savage current that ran all through her. She screamed into his mouth, a cry she didn't even recognize as her own.

Her body clamped down like a vise on his. He roared and splashed his come deep into her, her pussy milking him with violent convulsions that had her mindlessly writhing and arching and bucking beneath him.

Tryton collapsed heavily onto her. Niki, still feeling the strong pulses of her climaxes rushing through her, could only manage a wordless gasp. The water fell lifeless again about them, puddling under their shivering bodies.

And he'd been right, she'd never been so clean in her life. In fact she was so clean, it was only her thoughts that were dirty…

Chapter Fifteen

The Egyptian night was cool and dark but for the pale light of the rising moon.

Niki tried not to feel self-conscious in her borrowed clothes—Tryton's—and black war paint that Cady had sworn would serve as good as any Kevlar armor as she painted it on Niki's flesh. It was difficult, but she managed. Instead, she focused on the moment at hand, pushing away her weariness and her discomfort. She and Tryton had only managed a few short hours of sleep and her nerves were on a finite edge.

Grimm and Emily took the team—Cady and Obsidian, Edge, Cinder and Steffy, and Tryton and Niki— to the base of the Great Sphinx. One minute they were standing together in Tryton's meeting room and the next they were here, making ready for the hardships that surely lay ahead.

That ancient and mysterious monument that had withstood centuries, baffling scientists and indigenous people for so long, seemed to be waiting for them, patient and timeless as forever.

Niki shuddered delicately and waited for the Travelers to make the first move.

"We could go in, but we don't know what awaits us there," Emily murmured.

"No doubt the Daemons have some idea that we know something by now," Obsidian pointed out.

"Through Raine, they have an advantage that has proven most fortuitous for them."

"I believe you are right, Obsidian," Tryton agreed. "We will move to a point closer to where Niki escaped. It should be far enough to avoid a direct ambush. We'll still be walking into their midst, but we won't be put upon so quickly, without warning."

"Stealth and planning are our best options here," Edge remarked.

"I don't like this, Cady," Obsidian told his wife sternly. "I don't want you fighting in your condition."

"Condition? What condition? I'm pregnant, not ailing. Shut up and stop worrying. I won't hurt our babe." She smiled up at him when he growled. Obsidian might not like it, but she managed to get her way just the same.

It was clear to Niki that these Shikars were well used to dealing with each other. More than accustomed to fighting side by side in the worst of conditions. She wondered what she could possibly do to aid them, and fidgeted uncomfortably. This sort of thing was completely above and beyond her capabilities. She'd never fought a battle before, not even close. How could she help them?

"Join hands." Grimm's voice was as dark and shadowy as his form.

They appeared, closely cramped next to each other, in the crude passageway where Niki had fled from the Daemon a little more than a day before. The Shikars looked at her for affirmation. Niki nodded, trying and failing to find her voice.

It was so dark she shouldn't be able to see much at all, but her new Shikar eyes seemed well-equipped for just such a purpose. "This way," she finally managed, moving to lead them deeper into the darkness.

"Wait," Cinder and Tryton both reached to pull her gently back.

Cinder stepped forth and raised his hand aloft. A bright flare in the darkness nearly blinded her, and when the spots ceased to dance before her eyes, she realized with a start that Cinder's hand was engulfed in flame. He was using his hand as a torch to light their way.

Tryton's hand remained on her arm. "Stay close to me," he whispered in her ear.

As if she was going anywhere without him.

They moved down the passageway single file. Cinder, Obsidian and Edge were in front, with Cady, Steffy and Niki in the middle. Tryton, Emily and Grimm brought up the rear. The passage was difficult, craggy and uneven. Slow going, even with the way illuminated. Niki didn't remember the tunnel being so precarious as this, but then she'd been running for her life at the time, so it was no wonder she hadn't noticed it until now.

The walls of the tunnel were crude stone, but smooth in places, as if it had been carved out by human hands.

Or some other kind of hands, given the circumstances. Niki shuddered.

They walked for long, laborious minutes. Niki's muscles and lungs should have been burning from the exertion, and she was astonished that they didn't. Three miles or more they covered and still she wasn't even winded, despite the difficulty of the trek. It was amazing. She knew she had her new Shikar abilities to thank for it, and Tryton had told her to expect such wonders as she grew accustomed to her new form, but feeling it firsthand…Niki hadn't realized just how *different* being a Shikar would be.

The tunnel veered off suddenly.

"We're almost there," Niki whispered, realizing where they were and fearing what might come next.

Cinder held his hand aloft for a long moment, stopping so that the entire group was made to pause. Then the flames went out, plunging them into startling darkness.

"I feel them," Cady murmured.

Niki remembered that Cady was a Hunter, able to track the Daemons by feel alone.

Oh, *shit*.

"Steady," Tryton warned them all.

"Stay close and on your guard," Obsidian echoed.

They surged forward as one, into a much larger area of the tunnel.

Violence and noise erupted around them.

Niki froze, stunned and terrified. Her Shikar eyes clearly saw what her mind and heart screamed at her to look away from. Shadowy forms, each a mockery of humanity, a grotesquery of life and existence, loped and charged at them en masse.

Daemons. Dozens of them. Perhaps—*probably*—more. All of them intent on one thing. *Killing*.

There was nothing Niki could do but watch as the chaos played out around her, though she would have traded years of her life to be able to blot out the horrific images.

"Look out," Niki called the warning as the monsters came at them, but the warning was unnecessary.

The Shikars blazed through their attackers like a knife through butter.

A Daemon charged directly for Cady, as if it had a long-standing grudge against the woman. Cady, calm as you please, raised her hand, in which she held a mini-Uzi. She sprayed a barrage of bullets into the Daemon until it fell at her feet. She pointed her finger at it cockily and it whooshed into flame. Cady stepped over it and moved on to the next Daemon, already fast approaching.

Grimm lifted his arms out from his sides, like Moses parting the red sea, and stepped forward into a mass of Daemons. He disappeared in their swarming midst. Oddly, each Daemon seemed to pause and still. A second passed. One Daemon wavered on its crooked legs, the rest seemed to do the same, and then they were crumbling one by one, like hell-spawned dominoes.

A thick, wet sound at her back drew Niki's attention. She looked behind her to see a mass of swollen, throbbing organs—Daemon hearts!—falling into a pile upon the ground. She gasped and stepped away, bumping into something solid. Grimm righted her easily, having appeared at her side. "Careful," he murmured, steadying her before he was off again.

Cinder streaked by, setting fire to the mass of hearts as he passed. From his outstretched hands spewed a never-ending river of fire. He looked like a living, walking flamethrower. Whatever Daemon dared to cross him ended up engulfed in flame, burning alive. Soon the cavern was no longer dark. Instead, it was brightly lit by all the burning Daemon bodies littered about.

A Daemon made a beeline for Niki and she looked about, but there was no place to hide. She felt her power, the burn of it, the wildness that she'd always feared, as if it had been waiting for her to notice it all this time. Desperately she fed that flame within, until it was ablaze. The Daemon had almost reached her…

She flung her hands out to protect her face from its razor-blade claws…and the monster fell dead at her feet.

Niki sobbed a broken breath and stepped over the corpse, running for the closest wall and putting her back to it defensively.

Another Daemon raced to attack her.

"Niki!" Tryton cried out her name.

And time seemed to slow.

The monster slowed its headlong flight. Its murky, flame-orange eyes widened as if in surprise. Its horrible flesh bubbled and undulated strangely, alarmingly. All of a sudden, a million droplets of moisture escaped from its skin. Like a strange, watery explosion, the water splashed out and over her. The Daemon's form remained standing only a second and then it crumbled into dust.

Tryton had removed the water from it, killing it instantly.

He was at her side immediately. "My goddess, my love, are you hurt?"

She shook her head, mute. He'd called her *love*.

"Stay here and don't—" he began, but Niki saw a Daemon at his back and shoved him away.

Lashing out with her power, not even knowing *how*, but doing it as if she'd done the same a thousand times before, she aimed all of her strength at the approaching danger. The Daemon gave a horrible roar and died, twitching as it fell to the ground.

Her power was stronger now, far stronger than she'd ever imagined it could be.

Tryton looked down at the fallen monster, not a little stunned at Niki's display. He turned to her and gave her a roguish wink. "That's my girl," he praised, kissing her mouth hard before he disappeared, back into the fray.

Niki looked about, just in time to see Edge run straight up the side of a wall before coming down with a violent swoop of his Foils, decapitating three Daemons at once.

Steffy, too, was using her foils. She was throwing them like boomerangs all about the room. They glinted blue, razor-sharp, and struck out to slice through numerous limbs, before arcing in the air and returning to her outstretched arms from whence they had come.

Obsidian was busy hacking away at a particularly large monster. It stood no less than ten feet tall, and was almost as wide. Niki stepped forward and threw her power out to aid him…the Daemon paused in its struggles and fell dead, with Obsidian's Foil-bedecked arm buried up to the elbow in its chest cavity.

The midnight-haired warrior turned to nod her way in thanks before disentangling himself and launching himself at the closest monster, slicing its head clean from its shoulders.

Emily appeared at her side, covered in the black muck of Daemon blood. "Are you all right?"

"Yeah, I'm fine." Niki marveled that it was true.

The fighting subsided around them and as the last monster fell, brought down by Tryton's neat water trick, Niki and Emily moved to join the group in the center of the cavern.

But no sooner had they regrouped than another, larger swarm of Daemons appeared.

"*Fuck*," Cady screamed as one of the Daemons' blows connected with her shoulder. She blazed her fire into the monster's eyes and it screamed. With a wild cry she pounced on her enemy, ripping its heart free from its chest with naught but the strength of her bare hands.

"There are so many of them," Steffy cried as she proceeded to cut several of the Daemons nearest her into ribbons.

"Stand away," Tryton called.

The Shikars moved in unison, making a path for their leader. Tryton raised his hands at his sides. A sudden, violent gust of wind preceded a deafening roar…it was a river of water!

An incredible rush of it swarmed from behind and over them, blasting the Daemons all at once. It flooded the cavern, rushing in from wherever Tryton had called it forth, decimating their enemies in one fell swoop. The Shikars were safe, the only ones in that flooding torrent who were, and as quickly as it had begun, the flood ceased. Only carnage was left in its wake. A massive pile of Daemon bodies had washed up against the cavern's walls, like a dam of lifeless driftwood.

"Burn them," he commanded and Cinder and Cady stepped forward to obey.

Light and heat engulfed the cavern.

"Where to next? We need to move quickly before they recoup," Tryton asked Niki.

Niki nodded to the farthest end of the cavern. "Over there. There's a boulder or a shelf of rock, I think. You'll know it when you see it."

Indeed they did. It was an enormously broad boulder standing no taller than five feet, nestled into a dip in the wall. Cinder's hand lit to torch their way again.

Obsidian stepped forward and smashed his hands into the stone and it shattered into a trillion fragments of dust and debris.

"That's one way of doing it, I suppose," Grimm noted. Niki wondered if it was possible that he might be a little bit petulant that he hadn't been called upon to Travel them to the other side of it. Petulant? Grimm? No way.

He seemed to notice Niki's attention on him and turned to face her, his features hidden by the depth of his black cowl. "What?" he asked, sounding more than a little defensive.

"Nothing." She smiled secretly to herself and stepped through the opening behind the boulder, one step behind Cady who now led the way.

A horrible, chilling sensation washed over her.

Something slimy and oily seemed to coat her skin, as if she'd just swum through a sludgy oil slick on water. A horrible, ghastly odor assailed her nostrils and she gagged. Her eyes watered and her lungs burned. "What was that?" she asked, frightened and disgusted.

"We've crossed a Gate of some kind — a back door into another dimension. We're in the Horde realm now," Tryton told her, keeping his eyes ahead of them, focused intently, it seemed, on their pathway in the dark.

They came upon a crossroad. The tunnel opened up to reveal several more tunnels, each leading off into another direction of impenetrable darkness.

"Which way do we go?" Cinder asked, holding his torchere-hand aloft to light their path as best he could.

"I don't know," Niki frowned.

"We can't explore all of them, and no *way* am I splitting up," Emily said firmly.

Cady seemed to freeze, lifeless, where she stood. Her body shuddered and she let out a long, deep sigh. "There's something this way," she moved towards one of the tunnels.

"Wait," Obsidian reached out to stop her. "More Daemons?" he asked.

She shook her head slowly as if in a fugue. "No, I don't think so," she murmured.

"Then what? Is it Raine?" Grimm moved like a shadow to her side.

"No, not her either." Cady turned her head this way and that, like a hound scenting the wind or listening for prey. "But something," she shook free from Obsidian's hold and trudged forward into the tunnel.

"Cady, wait," Obsidian called.

But she didn't listen. Her footsteps echoed back to them as Obsidian sighed and moved to follow her. Niki and Tryton and all the rest followed too, and the darkness swallowed them up, despite Cinder's brightly burning hand.

Chapter Sixteen

The air wasn't so moist and rotten here. The stench of it was far less fetid and strangely enough, considering they were so deep underground, it suddenly felt warmer. The farther they moved, the cleaner the air seemed to become, and soon they are all breathing easily once again. Niki sighed her relief. It echoed for an eerie moment about the cramped passageway before fading into nothingness.

"We are below the Sphinx now," Grimm murmured.

"Yes," Tryton agreed easily enough, but Niki wondered at his tenseness as he walked by her side in the darkness. "I feel it too," he murmured. His agitation and concentration were palpable on the air between them. She took his hand in hers and squeezed it in hopes of somehow soothing him. She gasped, alarmed at how cold his skin had gone. When she turned to ask him what was wrong his fingers clenched tight about hers, as if to warn her to keep silent for the moment.

Something was amiss. Niki knew it, *felt* it in him. She could hear it in his breathing and his heartbeat. Something wasn't right here. But what could it be?

"Tryton?"

"Shh," he hushed her, squeezing her fingers impossibly tighter in his, never once glancing her way.

"It's this way," Cady said, quickening her pace. "I can feel it, stronger now."

"I've been too selfish," Tryton murmured.

Niki frowned and tripped over a ridge in the floor.

But it wasn't a ridge at all. It was a doorway. An elaborately carved Egyptian cover stone was nestled deep in the ground. It led the way to an immense, perfectly rectangular doorway carved into the wall of the passageway. Niki crossed it, hot on the heels of everyone else, and was floored by what she saw awaiting them beyond the threshold.

The passageway opened into an incredibly vast room of columns and statues—all in the ancient Egyptian style— that seemed to stretch on forever. The ceilings and columns stood hundreds of feet high at least. Cinder's illumination barely reached halfway upwards to light it, but there were other, as yet unseen sources of illumination that caused the great room to glow a soft amber hue.

"What is this place?" Emily asked on an awed whisper of breath.

"This way," Cady began trotting across the vast room and they all followed her faithfully.

Niki looked ahead, far ahead, to a deep pocket of shadows. As their group raced toward it, Tryton began lagging behind, pulling her back, as he would not release her hand.

"Tryton, *come on*," she pulled at him.

"Don't hate me," he said, surprising her.

"What?" She frowned. "What are you talking about Tryton? You're not making any sense."

"I've been a fool," he said with stunning fervency. "I've held back from you, fighting against fate. Fate is inevitable. There is no escape."

"What's the matter with you?" she gasped, worried.

"I love you," he said, shocking her to her toes. "I do. I loved you from the first moment I saw your sweet face. I have a heart. I have loved for centuries—that's why I've made so many mistakes, that's why I've been so selfish and secretive all these years."

"I love you too." She smiled through her tears and tried to tug him along—the others were getting far ahead of them now. "Come on."

"I had to tell you, before this. Before the end—"

"End? What end? This is a beginning. Now come on, I want to see what's ahead. Maybe Raine's waiting up there for us to save her."

Tryton pressed a hard kiss to her mouth. "I won't lose you," he vowed.

"I'm not going anywhere," she promised, and this time when she tugged on his hand, he followed her. They broke into a run to catch up with the team and Niki's heart was racing—but not from exertion.

He loved her!

She'd been right all along. She'd known he loved her. And now, finally, he knew it too.

No matter what he feared might happen, she swore to herself that she would do everything in her power to keep that love safe. He was hers, her man, her one true love— nothing could change that. *Nothing.*

They ran for what felt like forever, just they two. When they caught up with the others, Obsidian was struggling to shove a round disk—another odd door covered with ornate hieroglyphics—out of its resting place in a wall. It was big and thick, made out of a shining black stone that looked suspiciously like…well, like obsidian.

"It won't budge," Obsidian gasped, as if surprised his strength hadn't been enough to move the disk.

Niki realized he must, indeed, be incredibly strong. Stronger than she would have guessed. She looked down at herself, wondering just how strong *she* might now be if she were to put her new Shikar body to the test.

"Let me help," Cinder moved forward to assist with the disk.

The two men strained and pushed and beat against it, but to no avail.

"I could just Travel us to the other side," Grimm said with no small amount of impatience.

Emily chuckled quietly.

Of a sudden, there was a bright, blinding flare of light from around the edges of the disk, illuminating it on all sides. Obsidian and Cinder both tripped backward in stunned surprise.

"Did you do that?" Obsidian asked, frowning fiercely.

Cinder shook his head. "No, that wasn't me."

There was a mighty shudder of the earth at their feet. A deafening rumble had them all clutching at their ears protectively, and thousands of years worth of dust motes swam about them like a tiny sandstorm, stinging their eyes. The walls trembled, the columns undulated alarmingly.

And then all was still.

"What the fuck was that?" Steffy exclaimed.

The ground shook again, more violently this time, and Niki shrieked her surprise. She kept her balance but only just, staying on her feet thanks mostly to Tryton's steady, unwavering hand clasped strong around her own.

"Don't hate me," he said again, softly.

She squeezed his hand as the world about them shuddered and rolled.

The earthquake fell still again, but Niki wasn't taking any chances that it would stay that way. She braced her legs far apart, ready and expecting another shift of the earth beneath her feet at any moment.

The light appeared behind the disk again and then—lo and behold!—it rolled easily off to the side, revealing a round, open doorway behind it.

The soft amber light inside beckoned them further. Cady led the way, with Obsidian directly behind. Next went Steffy and Cinder. Then Edge and Emily. The Traveler paused before stepping through, looking back at them through the shadows of his cowl.

"The time is now Elder," he said enigmatically.

"I know," Tryton answered.

"I will stand by you always," Grimm promised formally.

"We have come full circle at last."

"You knew it would come to this one day."

Tryton nodded. "I knew. I feared it, but I knew."

"You did what you thought was right," Grimm assured him with quiet vehemence.

Niki looked questioningly from one man to the next.

"But I was wrong," Tryton said, gritting his teeth against the admission. "I let it go for too long."

"You don't know that yet," Grimm said.

"Come on," Niki said softly. "Whatever you're dreading isn't going away, so let's go face it together."

Tryton looked at her, surprised. Then, miraculously, he smiled. "You are a goddess," he said.

Niki laughed. "I'm glad you noticed. Now come on." She wouldn't take no for an answer this time. She dug in her heels, tugged his arm hard, and stepped ahead of Grimm, crossing through the doorway. Ready to face what lay beyond with her true love at her side, she stepped across the threshold.

Into the soft amber glow of the future.

It took a moment for Niki's eyes to adjust to the light, but when they did she was not a little surprised by what she saw.

This room was smaller, more the size of Tryton's meeting room—indeed it wasn't too unlike it at all, cozy and welcoming. It was empty but for a few stone benches, some brightly glowing torches perched in mounts on the walls, and beautiful hieroglyphic carvings and paintings upon every available surface. And a simple, stone throne.

Upon which a blond-haired man sat, silent and unmoving.

At his side stood a tall, straight man with broad shoulders and narrow hips. He wore a cloak and hood, so his features were hidden for the most part, but Niki could see the orange-yellow glow of his Shikar eyes burning out as he watched them.

Cady frowned and approached the throne, unafraid. "*You.*"

The man in the cloak stepped away from the throne, coming to meet her. Obsidian growled and stepped between them. Cady grunted and tried to push her husband aside, but he would not budge.

"I don't understand," Cady said around her husband, to the man. "What's going on here? Why do we keep running into you?"

The man reached up.

Obsidian's Foils made an ominous *schnick* sound as they erupted from his forearms threateningly.

The man paused then, more slowly, reached up to push back the cowl hiding his features.

Cady, afforded her first good look at the man, screamed on a gasp. "No! It's not possible..."

Tryton let go of Niki's hand and took a step forward, approaching the throne, as Cady, Obsidian and the cloaked man eyed each other. Tryton moved towards the other, the blond man, whose shining head was bent, his features shadowed and unmoving. He could have been dead for all Niki could tell. He was still as stone, seemingly oblivious to his surroundings, silent and lifeless as the grave.

Tryton stood before him, taking that one last step that would put him within arm's reach of the blond statue...when the man moved.

His head lifted. The light hit his features, illuminating his face.

Niki's gasp was lost in the echo of everyone else's. Everyone but Cady's, that is. Her eyes were still locked with the other stranger's.

The man's face...it was Tryton's.

The two looked so much alike. But for their hair— Tryton's was more gold than this strange man's—they could have been twins.

The man stood, dust motes dancing off of him with each movement, as if he hadn't moved from his perch upon the throne in centuries. He smiled stiffly, as if the expression was alien to him.

He looked so much like Tryton. Niki looked from one to the other, confused and stunned, as were the other Shikars.

The man spoke at last, his voice metallic and ancient and chilling…but oddly compelling. "Hello, brother."

Tryton nodded slowly. "Hello, Daemon."

Lord Daemon, scourge of the Alliance, leader and creator of the Daemon Horde opened his arms in welcome.

And Tryton stepped into his embrace, returning it with a fervor that stunned them all.

...And there were voices and thunders and lightnings and there was a great earthquake, such as was not since men were upon the earth, so mighty an earthquake, and so great... And every island fled away, and the mountains were not found – Revelations

Chapter Seventeen
The long ago past…

He smiled, watching his younger—by only a few moments—brother play with the primitive peoples along the shoreline. He moved his hands over the sand, watching with excitement as it swirled and moved. Seconds later, a beautiful flower bloom appeared, an exquisite sculpture of glittering earth.

There came a shriek from the shore and he darted his head up to see one of the primitives fall back, clutching at her foot and weeping.

He raced down to her. He soothed her as best he could with his words, but these strange beings that looked so much like his people and were yet still so different, had no understanding of language. He shushed her, looking at where the jellyfish had stung her foot. The girl continued to weep, but not so loudly now—thank the Fates, he hated to hear a female weeping—and he called over to his brother.

"Here," he instructed, when his brother dropped to his knees beside him. Taking his sibling's hands to lay them upon the girl's foot, he coached softly, "Do it just as Mother showed you."

The boy who looked so much like him smiled, eager to practice his new skill as he was eager to practice all things Shikar. He turned to the girl, laying his hands on her foot. He grunted in concentration, a few minutes passed in silence as he worked the magic, and then she was healed.

"Good work," he praised his brother, feeling like a god when the girl hugged them both in thanks.

* * * * *

Flash forward…

"Mother says we are not to love them," his brother warned him.

But he knew a way to love them without killing them. And now that he knew it—an older male had given him the secret—there was *no way* he was going to deny himself such pleasures as could be had with the human women. "I never said I wanted to love them. I just want to fuck them." He chuckled and it was an earthy sound, even to his own ears.

"It is not wise."

"You are always too conservative, my brother, my love," he scoffed. "You will end up being the oldest virgin in history if you keep this up."

"I just have a feeling," his brother said, frowning at the rebuff. "I do not think it wise that you go down this path."

"Are you having visions now like The Seer?"

"No, but I just—"

He snorted. "I want that one." He pointed to a lithe redhead as she worked in the field, gathering berries. "She has legs so long," he shuddered, feeling himself grow hard as stone. "I could wrap them around me twice."

The girl looked up, noticing him as all the maids did. She smiled, a come-hither look in her simple brown eyes.

He smiled back, and left his brother in the dust as he ran up to join her.

The call of his name on his brother's lips echoed behind him. He never looked back...

* * * * *

Flash forward...

"You cannot teach them our words."

He started and turned to see his brother behind him with a stern, disapproving look marring his handsome features. He sighed and turned back to the group of humans who were eagerly awaiting their next lesson. "You, always with a warning on your lips. I see no harm in this."

"You never see any harm in anything," his brother said in exasperation. "But it is forbidden to teach them our words. It has always been. They are not Shikar. They are not like us."

"Go away and leave me to my own devices. Don't you have a lake to make or a river to redirect somewhere?"

"Stop this now, it can go nowhere! You cannot teach them our words."

"Just watch me." He frowned and intensified his efforts to teach the primitive peoples a way to communicate that involved more than grunts and gestures...

* * * * *

Flash forward...

Her skin was lovely and black and smooth. The black tattooed line about her eyelids gave an incredible, exotic slant to her beautiful, almond-shaped eyes. Her linen dress blew in the warm breeze, revealing a lush, full shape that would have shamed any Shikar female.

One look at her as she walked in the harvest procession, the breeze teasing the lovely black locks of her ceremonial wig, the lotus petals flying from her hands as she tossed them about, and he knew that he was lost.

He had to have her.

It took many months to woo her. For the first time he'd felt the weight of time like a burden on his shoulders, he who had never even really noticed its passage before. It had been so long a time to him, these months of chasing her.

Though he was a god here, she was yet a maiden, and a worshipper in one of the temples. To take her would be to take her status in the temple, to insult and degrade her. After being touched by a man—even a god such as he— she would no longer be fit to dwell within the holy place. Her people required of him a ceremonial mating, a bond promised to her in the eyes of law and custom and religion.

He hated how people manipulated religions to suit their own needs and agendas. But in this instance, perhaps for the first time in all his life, he was willing to follow the rules. For her.

To a point.

It had been hard—indeed *he'd* been quite hard since the very moment he first laid eyes on her—but he managed it somehow. It was the longest he'd ever taken to woo and win a woman, but the wait and the fight only seemed to make the winning all the sweeter.

He had claimed her as his goddess. His beautiful and perfect Litha. And tonight he would claim her as his, make her his queen.

And Fate willing, he would make her a Shikar.

He was sure he could do it. He'd been working on animals and fish for centuries now, out of curiosity and boredom. How could he have known all this time that these experiments were merely a preparation for the real thing—for *this* one woman?

Gods, how he loved her! How he wanted her. In her he saw all the good things he knew he could be and do. Her soul shone bright like a beacon, pulling him and luring him and proving to him that he'd been right all this time in thinking that there was something infinitely special about humans, despite their flaws and weaknesses. There was something so special and amazing about this one woman that outshone even the most favored and adored Shikar female.

And tonight she would be his forever. He would see to it.

He whistled as he walked through the palace. A palace he himself had designed. Indeed he was responsible for everything around him, in some way or another. Without his aid, humans would have never gotten this far and he knew it.

Everyone knew it by now. Though he hadn't wanted the humans' thanks, he was quite enjoying the benefits of being worshipped as their god. Not their one true god— while he had no belief in a true god, he had his suspicions, and wasn't one to taunt the powers that might or might not be—but he was worshipped as a god all the same. Didn't he deserve it, after all? For all his hard work and dedication to these beings, these humans, who were really only strangers on their world?

No. He wouldn't think that way anymore. His woman would not like such thoughts, he felt sure. No. He must work on his arrogance, get it out of the way and get on with loving her and her people for who and what they were. Fragile and newborn they might be, but they were a part of his world. His woman's world. He would learn to think differently of the humans, he must.

Damn it, his brother had been right all along. He grinned. He hated it when his brother was right. It was just so often that he was...he should have listened to the warnings.

But if he had listened to reason all this time, then he wouldn't be here now, on his way to his marital chamber within the palace. Indeed, none of these temples and statues and palaces would even exist if not for him. And neither would she...his woman, his love, his mate.

He'd helped make it all possible. He and, in no small way, his twin brother had brought it all to pass.

He entered the doorway that would be the entrance into his future...his bride awaited.

Litha welcomed him into their bed with outstretched arms.

"My Lord Geb," she called to him.

He winced. He'd been called many names over the eons. Amun, Heh—those were the most recent and not the most significant. He had done nothing to halt the progression of names, of titles and labels, for they'd meant nothing to him. People would call him what they wanted, for he'd never given his true name, and he had no cares about it. Until now.

"Call me Daemon," he whispered to her, leaning into her upon their soft lovers' bower.

"Daemon," she sighed, helping him remove his vestments and jewelry.

She unbraided his long blond hair—done now in the style of her people—stroking her fingers against his scalp as she freed each long lock.

"Tell me you love me," he pleaded.

"I love you, My Lord," she said, and it was tragic that he had to ignore the blind, religious fervency in her voice. The love she professed, was it for him as a man or for him as a god and her royal superior? He would not dare think on it.

He would make her love him. *Him*, Daemon. The man, not the god. He vowed it to himself and to her.

Daemon closed his eyes and let her hands work their magic in his hair. Dragging her scent deep into his lungs, he let the love he felt for her flood through him completely, warm and safe and beautiful. He'd never been so truly content as he was here, in this one gentle moment.

Now he knew, there could be no doubt, that he had been waiting for this moment his entire life. And all of it had, indeed, been worth the wait. Worth the effort, worth the risk.

He rolled her in the sheets and pillows, reveling in her soft, nude skin. Her legs were smooth and plump. Her belly was a rounded mound of downy softness. Even the shaven baldness of her scalp—skin bared to more comfortably carry her ornate wigs—was perfect and beautiful wholly feminine. Her breasts were sweet and large and full. Her nipples long and hard and perfect.

Daemon moved down her body, impatient love and anticipation built up to a boiling point. Though he wanted to make it last, he feared he might yet lose control.

"My love, my love," he breathed between her legs, tasting the salty sweet essence of her with a glad rush in his heart. Here, the perfume of her—herbs and incense and womanly musk—was stronger, making him dizzy and weak with animalistic hunger.

He rose over her, looking down into the limpid dark pools of her eyes and hooked her legs around his back.

"Tell me again that you love me," he demanded.

"Yes, My Lord," she panted, eyes glazed with passion.

Unable to wait another moment, he came into her, rending her maiden's flesh so that she cried out and scratched at his back. How he wanted to lose himself in her. But he loved her, so he made it last. He held himself back as long as he could, stroking his cock in and out of her until she was moaning and crying beneath him.

He worshipped her face with his kisses. Worshipped her body with his, and gloried in each and every response he wrung from her. Every sigh, every moan and groan and sob, he took into himself like sacred treasures to hold and save forever.

The earth shook about them—his iron hold upon his powers was slipping—and a crack appeared in the floor beside their bed. Daemon closed his eyes and sank into her with a fierce thrust of his hips that made the lands of Egypt quiver and shake. Litha came with a surprised cry, her pussy squeezing him with merciless, rhythmic spasms that made him want to scream his lust and excitement aloud.

"Brother, don't do it," a voice cried at his back.

But it was too late. It had been too late the first moment he'd seen her...

He let himself go, wanting so much to have her, hold her, make her his completely. He came with a groan, shuddering over her. Filling his woman, his Litha, with his seed, his essence, his love.

His poison.

"*No*," Tryton screamed, agonized to witness Daemon's fall.

Litha, his woman, his one, gasped and went limp in his arms.

But Daemon was not worried. He would bring her back, he knew he could.

"Daemon, stop, you don't know what you're doing!"

"Leave me be, brother," he growled. "Go back to your ocean kingdom, your Atlantis, and let me rule here in peace for once! I have all well in hand here."

"You don't understand. This won't work—"

"Silence," he roared, hating the cool feel of Litha dead in his arms, but still confident that he could bring her back.

Tryton came and sat on the edge of the dishabille that had been his marital bed and clasped his shoulder in a strong, supportive grip. "I will aid you as I may," he offered.

Daemon smiled, never so thankful as now for his brother's never-ending loyalty and strength. Tryton may be trying to him at times with his scholarly ways...but Daemon loved him, despite it. Or perhaps because of it.

Daemon's hands were shaking. Litha's flesh was growing colder by the minute...time was weighing on him. His love needed him and he must go to her...

"Hold her. I'll be back," he said and disappeared, Traveling to that other side — that strange realm where human souls wandered before moving on to their proper destinations across eternity.

Her scent and her taste were still with him, the feel of her on his skin and in his mind. He searched for her, certain that he could track her easily enough. Doubtless, she would have waited here for him, in confusion but with all faith that he would save her. He looked and looked...

But she was nowhere to be found.

He searched everywhere, for time immeasurable, calling out her name, screaming it when there was no answer, no response, no trace of her to be found...

When he finally returned, the palace was no longer there. Indeed, it seemed that time had sped up. Forty years had passed here on the plane of the living. Egypt had moved on without him. There were more temples now. More gods with his face, and even more without. There was glory and there was riches.

But — such sorrow! — there were also more slums, more poverty, more filth. More disease and dissent. He had not been here to save his children from their follies and their fragility.

Somehow, he couldn't find the strength to care too much. Nothing mattered to him anymore but...

He went in search of his Litha's remains, ready to try one last desperate attempt to bring her back to him. And when he found her, a wrapped bundle of linen in a stone mausoleum...he wept for all that he had lost. All that he had destroyed.

But no — he may save her still. He must. He would.

Calling to her, he gave her form all the strength he possessed to give, calling her back from the grave. Back from death.

"Please, Litha, my love, my heart," he wept.

How flawed he was. How wrong he had been all this time.

Litha awoke and his heart rejoiced. He held her to him, mindless to the changes in her, the *wrongness* of her. When he pulled back, he gasped and staggered back, away from the demon he had wrought from the flesh.

It wasn't Litha...it was a *thing*. A monstrosity. A beast wrought of old flesh and dust and bone and death. There was no soul, no mind, no feeling there within her. There was only hunger...a hunger he understood, even as it terrified him. That he could have created this—he screamed his failure and his pain to the heavens and the cry echoed out over all the lands.

When he killed Litha a second time, he lost what was left of his sanity and fell into the abyss of lonely, raving madness.

* * * * *

"You interrupted me, brother. This is all your fault," he spat at Tryton.

"Daemon, where have you been all this time?" Tryton exclaimed as his brother appeared within his home.

"If it hadn't been for you, your coming between us that night, I could have reached her in time."

Tears flooded Tryton's eyes, those golden orbs full of such pity and pain and understanding. Daemon hissed and turned away from the sight of them.

"Humans are more complicated than rabbits or fish or serpents. You should have known that. You might be able to resurrect animals but not humans. Not Litha."

"Don't you dare say her name!"

Tryton shied away from Daemon's rage. And well he should have. All Daemon could think of anymore was revenge. Revenge and killing and then, blissfully, his own death.

The ground split around the room, and Tryton's home rocked on its foundation with bruising, roaring violence.

"It's your fault she's dead," Daemon shouted over the din.

"No. No, I never wanted that. I meant only to warn you," Tryton protested. "The human body and heart are not so easy to call back from the abyss. It takes so much love—"

"See what your meddling has wrought, damn you," Daemon spat, unwilling to listen to more, and Tryton's humble house exploded about them.

The great island of Atlantis rocked on its foundation. Hundreds of people ran from their homes as the Earth surged beneath them, frightened and alarmed, each wondering what was amiss in their perfect kingdom on the sea.

Daemon raised his arms and called upon all his strengths. Graveyards opened up about the land. Earth and flesh and bone and death combined, until an army of deformed beasts walked the night, intent only on feeding their insatiable hungers for energy, raw and bright. Energy that only humans could provide...

People died. Everywhere. And the Earth surged into chaos. Mountains crumbled. Islands fell.

"Stop it, Daemon," Tryton screamed, seeing the destruction caused by Daemon's pain, feeling it all through the world like a wound open and bleeding. "You don't know what you're doing!"

But Daemon was lost in his madness and his heartbreak and there was no turning back for him.

Atlantis trembled beneath them. Tryton, seeking only to save his brother now, used his power to combat and overwhelm Daemon's.

The seas surged and drowned out the monsters Daemon had brought into being across the world. A flood of rain washed down to cleanse the land of the dead and rotting golems he had raised, but sadly, not all of them were felled.

Tryton felt his failure echo back to him over the miles of the world.

And so he tried harder, flooding the Earth with his efforts, even as Daemon tore the land apart with his.

He went to his brother and took him in his arms amidst the chaos. "I love you, Daemon. Do not let yourself be lost to me…let your woman rest. Let your love for her live on forever in memory. Give her and yourself peace."

Earth and Sea met in a horrible crash that ate the world. Atlantis fell, sinking beneath the surging waves.

The world shattered and was reshaped, overwhelmed with the ravages of the might and power Tryton and Daemon unleashed upon it.

Daemon felt his brother's arms around him, but he could not let her go. His Litha. Forever dead, forever gone. He slipped against the current of Tryton's love, unable to grasp it and save himself…

"I sought to kill my pain," he whispered. "But here I have given birth to more... You should never have come between me and Litha." He let go of Tryton and fell into the abyss that waited for him, the darkness and the quiet, the captivating endlessness of insanity...

Tryton's last words faded to an echo in his mind.

"I'm sorry, Daemon..."

But truth to tell, Daemon no longer blamed him, his apology had been unnecessary, his guilt unfounded. It hadn't been Tryton's fault, any of it. No. Daemon blamed himself...his arrogance and his pride had made him a fool. All that was left to him now was pain and grief and rage — at himself.

Eternity swallowed him whole, in his lonely, unforgiving grief, and his brother was gone from him.

Chapter Eighteen

"What will we do with them?" Emily asked Obsidian softly.

It seemed a time for softness. Here, back in the Shikar realm, with the infamous Lord Daemon held within a prison awaiting punishment, time and reality seemed a little fuzzy at the moment.

"I do not know," he admitted finally, wearily.

"He's paid enough, I think," Steffy said, echoing all of their thoughts. "It's not his fault that the Daemons got out of control. He withdrew all support from them once he found Lazarus."

"Yes, Lazarus..." Edge mused. "How astonishing that we should all have such tangled fates as this."

"I never knew Tryton had a brother." Cinder sighed heavily. "I never would have guessed that he kept such a past as his a secret...he is truly an immortal."

"He is our leader still. He has not changed. I will follow whatever path he commands us to take next. The Council can go off themselves for all I care—"

"The Council hasn't decided where they stand on these issues yet. Do not judge them too harshly too soon," Obsidian warned.

"But the Council will no doubt command Tryton to destroy Daemon. After all, whether he intended to or not, Daemon is directly responsible for the Horde War, the Daemons, all of it. And after they have passed judgment onto Daemon, they'll do the same with Tryton for all his deceptions. The Council can be unforgiving—they might even go so far as to banish Tryton."

"Banish him from the world he built after the cataclysm? I don't think so, Edge." Emily shook her head. "Antiquated and stern the Council may be, but without Tryton there is no Council, no Shikar world at all. We need him, now more than ever before. Surely they will see this as well, and act accordingly."

"But Daemon will be executed," Edge insisted.

Emily sighed heavily. "I hate this. All of it. It's just too much. I don't want Daemon dead—I never thought I'd say that about the Lord of the Horde himself, but there it is. He has punished himself enough over the years. And he never meant for the Daemons to thrive as they did."

"In my opinion he more than redeemed himself with the resurrection of Lazarus," Steffy said. "It's too bad that he learned the secret of resurrection—the combination of psychic power and pure love—too late. But it is good that he learned it with Lazarus, and that he healed a little because of it."

"How does Cady feel about all of this?" Cinder asked, looking about for her.

Obsidian frowned, realizing that she was missing. "Where is Cady?"

"Oh shit," Edge spat.

"No. She wouldn't." Obsidian's eyes widened and his heart sped up double time as he realized, of all people, she would be the one to dare whatever she wanted.

"Oh hell," Cinder said with a slow smile.

They rose as one—Obsidian, Edge and Emily, Cinder and Steffy—and made for the door.

* * * * *

Cady reached for the enchanted latch on the cage. A cage Grimm himself had fashioned to hold monsters, imbuing it with magic unimagined to prevent any and all escapes.

But as her fingers fell upon the lock, it opened of its own volition and she gasped, stepping back. Daemon stepped through, towering over her as he emerged from the prison.

"Stop it, Father," Lazarus called from behind him.

Daemon, his movements as slow as the glaciers over mountains, turned to his son and nodded. He stepped away from Cady and looked about the room as if only just rousing from a deep sleep.

"He's not your father," Cady snapped at him.

Lazarus smiled at her. "He is the only father I know. The father of my flesh, if not my soul."

"You look so much like Dad. You don't need to remember him, Armand, all you have to do is look in the mirror."

Lazarus put his hands around her upper arms, shaking her gently. "I am your brother in spirit, but my love and my life I owe to my father. Daemon gave me a new birth, a new beginning. He killed the Daemons who ended me and resurrected me from their ashes to live again, flesh of his flesh, blood of his blood. He took the pain of my death from me and raised me free of worry and disease and weakness. I have no real memory of my life before he came into it. He is my father now."

"He made the Daemons that killed you, don't you see that?" Cady ignored Daemon's eyes on her as she spoke to her brother—a brother she'd thought long dead and buried. Her heart had broken and mended so many times tonight she didn't know what to feel, what to think, what to do. On the one hand she was grateful to the Lord of the Horde for the return of her brother, but on the other she hated him for taking him in the first place.

"He has paid, so much you cannot guess," Armand—Lazarus—told her. "He never meant for our family—or anyone else—to die at the hands of his mistakes. Long before saving me, he had turned away from all the experiments, the trials, error after error. Indeed, he sat unmoving in his crypt for centuries before he felt my death through his bond with the remaining monsters. He shook himself free of lethargy and undeath to save me from my own and raise me to be strong, as his son. He does not deserve your condemnation. He has condemned himself enough already."

Cady shook her head, letting the tears fall. "I missed you so," she whispered.

"I watched you. I knew you. Father never let me forget you."

She swallowed hard and caught her breath, schooling her emotions. "I want you to stay here, with me and my family. I want my son to know you. I want my future babe to know you. I want to learn all about you and your adventures," she smiled through her tears.

Lazarus nodded. "I would like that very much."

Cady turned from him and looked at Daemon, so still and so unreachable even as he watched their reunion in silence. "I know how you can reclaim your place among our people," she told him.

Finally a response. Daemon frowned his question.

Cady smiled and nodded. "I promise, when you return, you'll be welcomed with open arms. Now hurry and listen," she cocked her head, "I can hear the others coming and I don't want them to stop you. Not yet..."

Chapter Nineteen

Tryton swept his hand down her throat, through the valley of her breasts, over her belly and down between her legs.

Niki moaned and thrashed beneath his seeking fingers. Her black skin gleamed like onyx in the light, covered in a thin sheen of moisture from their bath—he'd left her wet in more ways than one—for more reasons than one. Her hair was a tangle of darkness on his pillows, her body a shadowy wonder of delight.

"Let me ease you," he breathed, rubbing his palm gently into the mound of her cunt.

"You mean *tease* me," she gasped, opening her legs wider to accommodate him.

"That too," he grinned mischievously. He traced one finger over her clit, pressing lightly.

A zing of pure sensation, like an electrical bolt, blazed through her body, from her head to her feet, making her toes curl.

"*Oh fuck*," she shuddered.

"I admit that *is* what I had in mind." He stroked her with his finger again, spreading the moisture of her sex over the swollen nub of flesh.

"Stop your damn teasing and give me your cock," she yelled, straining beneath him.

"As you command, my goddess," he growled. With one swift, hard, deep stroke he came into her, slamming balls deep inside of her wet, welcoming pussy. "Always and ever as you command."

Niki screamed and clawed at his back, biting his shoulder as he began pumping his hips in and out of her.

"Gods, I love you so much," he gasped, raining kisses down all over her face and throat and breasts.

"I love you too, now *bruise* me." She slapped his bottom impatiently, smiling through gritted teeth.

Tryton laughed and increased the power and frequency of his thrusts. His cock stretched her tight flesh. Wet, slurping noises echoed in their ears with every stroke. Niki's breasts bounced, Tryton's hair flung about, and the bed groaned a loud protest with the abuse.

They rolled in the sheets, over and over, until she was riding him. Her thighs were tight around him, her weight a lush and welcome burden. Tryton groaned and strained up into her, feeling for her heart through the reach of his cock. He bounced her wildly on him, bucking and rocking into the wet, drowning heat of her.

Her hands kneaded the planes and ridges of his pecs, holding on to him with her fingers and her nails as she enjoyed the ride of her life. Her pussy felt deliciously bruised and burned by his thrusts, her bottom sore as she rose and fell upon him. Her breasts were heavy and stinging, bouncing in his face as he slurped voraciously and noisily at her nipples.

Niki grasped at his hair, pulling it, and Tryton rolled them in the bed, flipping her beneath him. He lifted her ass to his face and buried his face down into her pussy. She screamed again and thrashed to escape the exquisite torture, but he held her fast and fierce. His tongue speared her deep, moving in her like his cock, filling her, tasting her, swallowing all of her cream with greedy suckles.

He flipped her again and shoved her knees up to her chest, sinking his dick down into her once more.

"Oh god, you feel *so good*," he groaned.

Her eyes rolled back in her head, her entire being consumed by unimaginable pleasure.

He pounded into her, over and over again. She came to the precipice of pleasure several times, but each time he held her back, ceasing his movements until she came back away from the edge of ecstasy. Soon she was pounding on his imprisoning arms, bucking wildly up against him with her hungry hips, begging him to fuck her, to love her, to make her *coooooome*!!!!

"Ohgodohgodohgod," she panted.

"Niki, my love, my woman, my everything, I never want this to end." He licked his tongue back and forth across her raw, parted lips. He was tireless and he was unstoppable. Thrusting and thrusting and thrusting and thrusting — it was never-ending.

Niki was screaming on every breath before he took pity on her and angled her hips just so, to reach that special, magical place deep in the well of her. His thumb rubbed circles over her clit, his hips pounded into hers and when she rose to the peak of pleasure this time, he let her fly out over the edge.

With one last thrust and swipe of his thumb against her clit, he fell on her, taking her breast deep into his mouth to suck it roughly. He pulsed hard inside of her, filling her with the scalding hot wash of his cream.

Her pussy throbbed and pulsed and milked him, but still the essence of his release flooded over her, wetting the sheets, bathing them, soft and hot and wondrous, awash across their skin.

"No matter what happens, we have each other," he vowed, gasping it into her ear as he began again to pump his sex, soft and gentle into hers.

Uncaring that they were sweaty and they were messy—indeed she loved feeling this way with him—she wrapped her legs tighter about his waist and welcomed each movement of his body on hers. "I'll never let you go," she promised him, clutching him tight with her entire body.

"We'll go to Jada and raise her as befitting the daughter of the gods," he smiled, pressing hot, hard kisses into her mouth. "She will want for nothing, and neither will you or any of your family."

"You either," she insisted. "No matter what comes. No matter what's happened, we are together and that's all that ever has to matter. No more worries, no more cares than that."

"I never knew I could love so much," he gasped, rocking into her. "I don't know why I fought it so hard. I love you more than life, more than death, more than anything that ever was or will be."

Niki grinned, feeling her heart spill over with happiness the likes of which she'd never known or ever hoped to feel. "All this talk, that's all you ever do," she chuckled. "Now shut up and prove how much you love me," she dared.

He did, much to their delight.

Epilogue

Grimm smashed his fist into another piece of furniture, sending splinters of it flying through the air with his rage.

Raine was still out there, trapped and hurt and at the mercy of the Horde. Those beasts—damn Daemon for his pride and his folly—had his woman!

He slammed into another piece of furniture—a chair Edge had carved for him not long after Emily's change from human to Shikar. The chair had meant much to him, but it crumbled to dust beneath his blows. He had no outlet for his rage or his pain…the clock was ticking and with each second he knew his Raine needed him more and more and *more* fiercely.

"So you're the one who has been hunting me all this time," came a voice from behind him.

He spun around to face Daemon. "How did you come to be here?"

"I will not be locked up unless I wish it," Daemon told him with that emotionless, metallic voice. "But if you must know, your Cady had a hand in sending me."

"Cady. She always meddles," Grimm said under his breath, eyeing his unwelcome visitor.

"She meddled on your behalf this time, Traveler."

"What do you want?"

"I want nothing. But the sister of my son wishes me to aid you and so I will. Your woman—this Raine—I can help you find her."

Grimm's eyes went wide.

Daemon smiled, lips stiff as if he did not smile often. "Yes. I can feel her." He tapped his heart with a forefinger. "Though I cut myself off from my creations, I can still feel them. And through them I can feel her. She is waiting for you to come. Will you follow me to her?"

"I hunted you for centuries," Grimm marveled, unable to accept that Daemon could find Raine so easily after he had tried so hard, "but you were only playing with me. I could not find you, because you did not will it. I should have looked beneath your ancient statue, your Sphinx. I should have known."

Daemon cocked his head to one side, movements slow and alien. "I didn't play with you," he frowned. "I was not myself. I am still not myself." He shook his head a little. "I felt you searching, but I did not want to be found yet. My son is the reason I came out of hiding, you have him to thank if you will."

"If you know so much, if you are so powerful, why didn't you destroy all of the monsters?"

"I didn't care enough," Daemon said simply. "Or I thought that I had already destroyed them. Take your pick of the two or come to your own conclusion and you'll know more than I. I lost myself for so long…"

"Tryton could have helped you, as he did tonight, healing you with his love."

Daemon's face was a mask of silence. "I wasn't ready," he said finally.

Grimm understood, to some degree, the methods behind Daemon's madness. He had loved and lost... Grimm was not so different in that respect.

"Very well. Help me find Raine." Grimm gritted his teeth. "Please."

Daemon smiled again. "Take my hand then."

Just this once, Grimm was content to let someone else show him the way.

For now.

Enjoy this excerpt from
Fetish
© Copyright Sherri L. King, 2004

"This is the first step of your journey." Violanti—how did she know his name? Had she asked? She couldn't remember now—gestured her forward towards a jade-green door.

"Your name is Violanti?" she asked stupidly.

A small, amused smile appeared upon the lush moue of his mouth. "Yes, and it sounds lovely on your lips."

"It sounds…is it Italian?" She frowned, puzzled that it should matter or that she was even remarking upon it.

The smile disappeared. His eyes glittered from green to silver to blue, making her dizzy. "It is," was his short answer.

"Oh." Forgetting almost instantly what they'd been discussing, she looked beyond him to the green door. "What's in there?" Curiosity like she'd never experienced before nearly overcame her shyness.

That smile of his again. Was it a practiced thing? It was so sensual that it should have been. No man should have such an alluring attribute, without having to work for it a little. "Follow me to find out." He opened the door and stepped inside. Aerin couldn't have stayed behind had she wanted to. And she halfway did. Whatever was waiting behind that door, it made her nervous.

Once she stepped over the threshold, Violanti closed the door softly behind her. Trapping her. Trapping them. Together.

The room was lovely. Not at all sinister or threatening, as she'd feared. Soft hues of jade, accentuated by warm and creamy vanilla, gave the room a soothing and inviting quality. The lush scents of vanilla and perhaps a little apple or pineapple, were thick in the room and flattering to the décor. It added to the comfort of the space.

The perfume lulled Aerin, enveloping her, beckoning and seductive. Violanti's hand at her back coaxed and eased her. She moved further into the room. There was another divan here, piled deep with silk, and emerald in hue. It was positioned before a wall, the only item of furniture in the room that was free of the jade and vanilla motif. Violanti led her to it gently, but firmly, and joined her there upon it.

A light came on somewhere behind the wall they faced, making it transparent. Aerin realized it was a two-way mirror. Behind it, lay another room identical to theirs. Only there were several people in it.

Aerin blushed furiously and looked away. The long, cool fingers of her escort grasped her chin and turned her face back to the scene before them. "Look at them, Aerin. There is no shame in it."

She couldn't help it. She had to look. The blush deepened, burning her neck and breasts hotly. "Do they know we can see them?" Was that her voice, breathless and faint?

He chuckled softly. It was like a whisper, that small laugh. But she felt it vibrate along her very bones. "Of course. It's what they want. It's why they chose that room. They are exhibitionists; it is their fetish to be watched by others, and the club provides this experience for them."

"Can they see us?"

"No. Do you want them to?"

"No!" she exploded. Then, more calmly, "No. I'd rather they didn't. I—I doubt I have an exhibitionistic fetish myself."

Again that amused smile. Amusement at her expense. For a second she both hated and feared that smile and all the mysteries that lay behind it. But the moment came and went, and she went straight back to being dazzled by him, and by the scene unfolding behind the mirror. "I question whether you know your own fetishes, Mistress."

"I told you not to call me that. It makes me uncomfortable."

"Even after being in your own skin the whole of your life, I can see you are uncomfortable there. Why should this be any different that you must take exception?"

She pulled back with a shallow, unsteady breath; surprised that he could both injure and anger her so completely and so swiftly. "You don't know me. You shouldn't make assumptions about people you don't know."

His eyes glittered dangerously. "You made the assumption that I was interested in you out of pity or obligation simply because you paid for your stay here, didn't you?"

She had. Of course she had. It was a safe assumption to make. More than safe.

He seemed to see her admission of it, perhaps in the look of her eyes or face. This Violanti was very observant. "So you are as guilty as I of assumption. And perhaps we are both wrong...no. That's not true. I say you are wrong about me. While I know I'm right about you." He spoke the last with an underlying tone that practically dared her to disagree.

Aerin couldn't disagree, nor could she pretend to. He was right. She was a stranger in her own skin, had always been, and it would ever be so. But that didn't mean she had to approve of his observation of the fact.

"I don't want to talk about this." She glanced at the mirror, what lay beyond it, then looked away. "I shouldn't have come here. I need to go now."

Again, he laid his fingers—the tips of two, no more—against the pulse that beat in her wrist. Had he made any more of a movement, she would have perhaps unearthed the strength to bolt. But, as before, his small gesture effectively stilled her.

"Back to that again? I'm sorry, Aerin. I was being uncouth, forgive me. But I can plainly see that, of all our patrons, you need Fetish desperately. You need the comfort and pleasure we can give. And we can help you to find that hidden self you've so long forgotten. The part of you that isn't afraid of your own sensuality. Of your own sexual appeal. You've buried it deep, but still it is there, waiting for discovery. Let us help you find it. Let *me* help you find it."

Enjoy this excerpt from
Beyond Illusion
© Copyright Sherri L. King, 2005

He stalked slowly around her and though the urge to keep eye contact with him was there, she refused to budge as he circled her. He was like a predator regarding its prey...right before it pounced. After circling her once more, he came to a stop behind her and—just as she was about to turn to face him—his hands fell upon her shoulders, cupping gently, but keeping her from turning to him.

"Just relax and trust me," he whispered in her ear, and again, the sound did not carry over the speaker system.

His hands kneaded her shoulders lightly, and against her will she felt her knees grow weak. He blew softly into the hair at the nape of her neck and she felt heat pool low and heady in her belly. One of the hands at her shoulders lifted and the tip of one finger traced lightly down her spine. Her breath caught and moisture gathered between her quaking thighs. That such a small touch should affect her so! It was surely a form of magic all its own, this man's very charisma.

"Now close your eyes, Ellie," he commanded in a seductive voice.

"If I close my eyes I'll miss the trick," she said with a cheeky grin.

"Oh, I promise you'll not miss *this* trick. I'll make it good for you, just close your eyes." His words had many other meanings, as Ellie was sure he was aware, and despite her better judgment she fell a bit more under his spell.

"Close your eyes—" his breath was warm at her ear " —and keep them closed until I tell you to open them."

She allowed her eyes to drift closed, fully prepared to be unimpressed with whatever trick he had up his sleeve.

There was a *whooshing* noise in her ears, then silence. A few seconds ticked by and she dared to open her eyes a small crack, to allow for a small peek at what Vincent was doing.

She let out a choked gasp, her eyes flying fully open.

Looking about the room with nothing less than total shock, she realized that she was no longer on the stage. She was in a dressing room…and she had no idea how she'd gotten there!

About the author:

Sherri L. King lives in the American Deep South with her husband, artist and illustrator Darrell King. Critically acclaimed author of *The Horde Wars* and *Moon Lust* series, her primary interests lie in the world of action packed paranormals, though she's been known to dabble in several other genres as time permits.

Sherri welcomes mail from readers. You can write to her c/o Ellora's Cave Publishing at 1056 Home Avenue, Akron OH 44310-3502.

Why an electronic book?

We live in the Information Age—an exciting time in the history of human civilization in which technology rules supreme and continues to progress in leaps and bounds every minute of every hour of every day. For a multitude of reasons, more and more avid literary fans are opting to purchase e-books instead of paperbacks. The question to those not yet initiated to the world of electronic reading is simply: *why?*

1. *Price.* An electronic title at Ellora's Cave Publishing runs anywhere from 40-75% less than the cover price of the <u>exact same title</u> in paperback format. Why? Cold mathematics. It is less expensive to publish an e-book than it is to publish a paperback, so the savings are passed along to the consumer.

2. *Space.* Running out of room to house your paperback books? That is one worry you will never have with electronic novels. For a low one-time cost, you can purchase a handheld computer designed specifically for e-reading purposes. Many e-readers are larger than the average handheld, giving you plenty of screen room. Better yet, hundreds of titles can be stored within your new library—a single microchip. (Please note that Ellora's Cave does not endorse any specific brands. You can check our website at www.ellorascave.com for customer recommendations we make available to new consumers.)

Discover for yourself why readers can't get enough of the multiple award-winning publisher Ellora's Cave. Whether you prefer e-books or paperbacks, be sure to visit EC on the web at www.ellorascave.com for an erotic reading experience that will leave you breathless.

www.ellorascave.com

Lady Jaided

The premier magazine for today's sensual woman

Lady Jaided magazine is devoted to exploring the sexuality and sensuality of women. While there are many similarities between the sexual experiences of men and women, there are just as many if not more differences. Our focus is on the female experience and on giving voice and credence to it. Lady Jaided will include everything from trends, politics, science and history to gossip, humor and celebrity interviews, but our focus will remain on female sexuality and sensuality.

A Sneak Peek at Upcoming Stories

Clan of the Cave Woman
Women's sexuality throughout history.

The Sarandon Syndrome
What's behind the attraction between older women and younger men.

The Last Taboo
Why some women – even feminists – have bondage fantasies

Girls' Eyes for Queer Guys
An in-depth look at the attraction between straight women and gay men

Available Spring 2005

www.LadyJaided.com

NEED A MORE EXCITING
WAY TO PLAN YOUR DAY?

ELLORA'S
CAVEMEN
2006 CALENDAR

COMING THIS FALL

THE
ELLORA'S CAVE
LIBRARY

Stay up to date with Ellora's Cave Titles
in Print with our Quarterly Catalog.

TO RECIEVE A CATALOG,
SEND AN EMAIL WITH YOUR NAME
AND MAILING ADDRESS TO:

CATALOG@ELLORASCAVE.COM

OR SEND A LETTER OR POSTCARD
WITH YOUR MAILING ADDRESS TO:
CATALOG REQUEST
C/O ELLORA'S CAVE PUBLISHING, INC.
1337 COMMERCE DRIVE #13
STOW, OH 44224

COMING TO A BOOKSTORE NEAR YOU!

ELLORA'S CAVE
2005

BEST SELLING AUTHORS TOUR

3. *Mobility.* Because your new library now consists of only a microchip, your entire cache of books can be taken with you wherever you go.

4. *Personal preferences are accounted for.* Are the words you are currently reading too small? Too large? Too...ANNOYING? Paperback books cannot be modified according to personal preferences, but e-books can.

5. *Innovation.* The way you read a book is not the only advancement the Information Age has gifted the literary community with. There is also the factor of what you can read. Ellora's Cave Publishing will be introducing a new line of interactive titles that are available in e-book format only.

6. *Instant gratification.* Is it the middle of the night and all the bookstores are closed? Are you tired of waiting days—sometimes weeks—for online and offline bookstores to ship the novels you bought? Ellora's Cave Publishing sells instantaneous downloads 24 hours a day, 7 days a week, 365 days a year. Our e-book delivery system is 100% automated, meaning your order is filled as soon as you pay for it.

Those are a few of the top reasons why electronic novels are displacing paperbacks for many an avid reader. As always, Ellora's Cave Publishing welcomes your questions and comments. We invite you to email us at service@ellorascave.com or write to us directly at: 1056 Home Avenue, Akron OH 44310-3502.